April 5, 2014

```
||||||||||||||||||||||||||||||
MW01518485
```

DUBLIN,

To: GOLSEN

Another Item completed
From my bucket list.
My next novel is
almost completed.

Enjoy......

[signature]

GHOST OF A CHANCE

a novel by

Ronald Robert Gobeil

Copyright © 2014 by Ronald Robert Gobeil
First Edition – March 2014

ISBN
978-1-4602-2946-0 (Hardcover)
978-1-4602-2947-7 (Paperback)
978-1-4602-2948-4 (eBook)

Produced by:

FriesenPress
Suite 300 – 852 Fort Street
Victoria, BC, Canada V8W 1H8

www.friesenpress.com

Distributed to the trade by The Ingram Book Company

Table of Contents

Dedicated to Susan for her assistance and patience in putting up with me during the writing of this story.

Prologue

Jazz Hogue was starting to wake up, and he was freezing. And it was dark. He had never experienced darkness or cold like this in his entire life. The only sound was the wind, which was starting to pick up. And it was snowing! To top all this, he had a terrific headache, a sore neck and—worst of all—he wasn't plugged in to his ever-present world of jazz. *What the fuck is going on?* He found that he was even wearing hiking-boots. He'd never even owned a pair in his life! His wrists were tethered with rope, and to his horror, he found that, somewhere along the way, he had pissed himself.

Jazz was starting to shake from the cold and the damp piss in his pants was beginning to freeze. He was starting to shake uncontrollably. His broken finger was still in a splint and hurting like hell! For the first time in his life, he was shit scared and afraid that he was going to die. *I don't deserve to die like this, do I?*

Hogue knew he had done bad things all his life, but he didn't deserve *this*. It just wasn't fair. He was finally starting to make it into the big time. He knew he had broken most of societies rules a zillion times over. He had robbed mostly old people during his youth, and had *enjoyed* beating on them; he always got off on that! As he got older, he started into the lucrative drug trade. He had some bad dudes working for him.

Where the fuck am I? His teeth were starting to chatter. Slowly, the darkness was fading and he started to see some of his surroundings.

He was surrounded by forest, and he could faintly hear the sound of running water. The rope leading from his bound wrists was tied around a huge tree. And about five feet up the tree, he thought he saw a piece of notepaper, held in place by a jackknife. With a huge effort, he got to his feet and made his way to the tree and tried to read, but Jazz had to wait for the light to improve, in order to make out the writing. He suddenly started to feel nauseated, bent over and heaved out the contents of stomach. This was repeated two more times, and he thought he would pass out. He finally recovered enough to straighten up and this time he could make out the neat block lettering on the note.

Hello Asshole!

How does it feel to be on the receiving end for a change? Read this carefully, and you may live to see another day. You are on an island surrounded on both sides by a deep river. Do not attempt to swim for it, as you will freeze to death. You are at one end of this narrow island. If you remove the knife that is holding this note, you will be able to cut yourself free and make your way to a small cabin built into the trees not far from here. Make your way to it, and let yourself in. Once inside, you'll find matches on top of the stove. Use these matches to light the wood inside the stove. Think you can handle this, asshole? Once you warm yourself, further instructions are on the small table next to the stove. Get going now!

Jazz didn't hesitate to follow the instructions, as he was getting colder by the second. He cut himself free, pocketed the note and the jackknife, and walked as quickly as the uneven ground allowed. He located the cabin after about five minutes. He walked up to the roughly built structure in a small clearing, and without hesitation, let himself in. The cabin was dark. The matches were located on the stove as promised. He groped for the stove's metal-hinged door, and with shaky fingers, was able to fire up the dry kindling inside. Warmth finally started to revive his nearly frozen body. He was alive, at least for now, and he was able to find the second note. It sat on a roughly hewn table, next to the stove, beneath a wind-up flashlight.

Chapter 1

In an alley behind south Seattle's worst tenements, a meeting was in progress between three men. The subject of the meeting was their next hit. Heading the meeting was a short, powerfully built man in his early thirties. His face was badly scarred and reflected a roadmap of his life. The scarring was a result of barroom fight involving a broken beer-bottle and being knocked out in the process. He awoke to find a wino doctor ministering his wounds. The wino had prevented infection by pouring whiskey into the deep cuts and wiped off the whiskey with a bar towel. His wounds were then taped over. The resulting infection caused him to go to a local hospital, but as he was penniless at the time, they refused to treat him.

It took weeks to heal, and he emerged from the experience with horrible scars that extended from his left ear to his chin. The scars changed his life, and he became bitter and mean as a result. He would fly into a rage when anyone looked at him the wrong way. He emanated hate, and people shunned him. He hated the merciless medical system and anyone associated with it.

No person alive had crossed him since. His name was Harry Blankford, commonly known as "Bear". One look at him and anyone would know why. He had yet to be accused of any crime, for he had become cunning, crafty, and dangerous—a treacherous badass.

The two men currently being addressed were listening carefully to his instructions. The only reason they worked for Blankford was because they were always well paid. Hell, they were afraid *not* to work for him! Carl Abbott and Crab Williams were good at what they did and were Bear's loyal thugs. Neither of the two was overly bright, but their killing ability was good enough to satisfy Bear.

Their target was a man who now headed Secure Security Sentries—its new director. His name was Arthur Piedmont.

The *why* was none of their business. The threat was always there to get it done. Do it right, or pay the consequences. They would follow Bear's instructions to the letter. The hit was scheduled at two a.m., five hours from now, and they knew exactly where Piedmont would be located.

The meeting came to an end and as usual, they would each leave separately, at five-minute intervals. Bear would be the last to leave. Ten minutes later, he was getting set to be on his way.

Five feet away, a silent figure waited, blending into the nearby wall, invisible to the naked eye. His timing had to be just right. He made his move, and there followed a quiet hiss. Bear felt a sting to his throat, and fell unconscious onto the dirty pavement. His assailant dragged him to a waiting Ford Explorer, hidden in the shadows a block away. Blankford was dumped unceremoniously into the back of the vehicle; the stranger entered the vehicle and drove away, completely undetected.

—

A few hours later, Carl Abbott and Crab Williams—or, C&C as they were known—crept silently behind s small booth, set in front of a large warehouse. Carl was carrying a Smith & Wesson SD40. Crab's weapon of choice was a Beretta 92. Both men were good shooters. They stood with their guns pointing toward the gravel road. They were waiting for Arthur Piedmont's arrival in his slate grey Lexus. Arthur was making his usual rounds, ensuring that his warehouse guards were safe and positioned correctly.

They could see the approaching lights of the vehicle. It was moving slowly in their direction. They were alert, focused on the oncoming lights and both held their guns at shoulder height, waiting for the oncoming target to stop and emerge from his car.

Three hundred feet from them, a man dressed in night camouflage, was aiming a Blaser R93 tactical rifle equipped with a Swarovski Habicht night scope and a custom designed silencer. He sighted in on the two targets. He was an expert marksman. He could see them in great detail. Carl would be his first target; he was slightly behind, and to the right of Crab.

His finger gently pulled the trigger, and the bullet silently blew away Carl's trigger finger—it just disappeared—and before Carl could emit a sound, the shooter repeated the exact shot to Crab's trigger finger. They both screamed at the same time, while staring unbelievably at their missing digits. They were bleeding profusely and almost in shock. They dropped their weapons and fled. The shooter let them escape.

Arthur slowly drove up to the booth, stopped the car, and calmly climbed out of his Lexus. He was joined a minute later by the camouflaged man, gun in hand.

"You let them go?" Arthur asked.

"They'll never shoot anyone again, I assure you," said Matt. "Losing their trigger fingers will stay with them a long while."

"That's a beautiful rifle," said Arthur. "Accurate?"

"Very. I only use it for special occasions."

Arthur Piedmont thought for a moment.

"The two tonight, were they the men who killed… my predecessor?"

"Those two had nothing to do with my dad's death. The man who killed my father is now in my hands and will be dealt with accordingly. How about some breakfast, Arthur?"

The breakfast spot Matt picked out was close to Seattle's Sea-Tac International Airport, which suited his needs for his next little endeavor. His unconscious guest in the back of his Explorer would sleep soundly for the next twenty-four hours.

They met at Ziggy's, Matt's favorite breakfast bistro, located on the corner of 34th Avenue and 176th Street, near the Airport. The specialty was omelets and huge mugs of the best coffee in Seattle. They placed their order with the friendly waitress, and with coffee pot in-hand, she filled their mugs and departed to place their order.

Matt Chambers was a natural-born leader. He was a lean six foot three and ruggedly handsome. Intelligent, private, successful, resourceful, and highly organized, Matt's Army background included defensive training, weaponry, camouflage and infiltration—which prepared him well for his present plan.

In business, he was a brilliant delegator.

His private passion was kept entirely to himself: To make a definite difference in the world by way of extreme measures, utilizing his past experience with the Army, his business acumen, and his sense of fair play.

His first priority was the safety and security of his family. The second was to continue his father's business, and the third was to make a success of the company he and his father had started.

They were settled quietly into one of the corner booths. Conversations between them had always been enjoyable. Arthur was an interesting man. He was in his early fifties, impeccably attired and always reminded Matt of a retired English Squire. He sported a neat, well-tended mustache, had piercing blue eyes—a lot of intelligence lurked behind those eyes. Arthur was born in England, where he attended Oxford intending to become a lawyer; however, this was not to be. He disliked the slowness of the legal system, as everything took too long, and clever well-paid lawyers usually managed to get charges dropped on mere technicalities. Judges were told by government to merely slap the hands of criminals because jails were filled to overflowing. The justice system was a joke, and the youth were laughing at authority. Rather than instant justice, English law was being bogged down by large backlogs of cases.

Arthur's second choice was the garment business, as it proved to be such a clean elegant way to make a living. He had met Herod Chambers at his shop and gravitated to his views and good business sense. Herod made Arthur a proposal, inviting him to join him in an up-and-coming business venture that was set to explode onto the world stage. After ten years in the garment business, Arthur was ready for a new challenge. He sold his clothing business to an associate and promptly moved to Seattle.

Waiting for their breakfast, a strange silence had fallen between them; Arthur was first to break it.

"How are you coping with your dad's death, Matt?"

"Better now, but I still miss him a lot. I mostly miss the camaraderie we had."

Matt remembered working with his father after leaving the Army. Together they had accomplished so much. Father and son had broken ground on a completely new concept. Security satellite surveillance was brand new. Three years previously, it had started out as a dream. However, tragedy had struck near the end of that dream. Herod was shot while making his usual evening inspection a year earlier, on September 4, at two thirty, on a cold Sunday morning. It seemed like only yesterday, and Matt had only the fondest of memories of his dad, his mentor, his best friend, and business partner.

Herod Chambers had previously founded, owned and managed a similar type of company, and it went by the name of Secure Security Sentries (SSS Inc). He was one of the pioneers of business security, but on a more basic system. Retired Army and Police personnel, who were well screened, were hired as his security guards. Everyone who worked for Herod had loved the guy. He was an excellent trainer, paid well and had allowed his employees to think on their feet. When they made mistakes, they were quickly corrected, but never chastised.

Herod's clientele loved both his methods and his fair pricing. Above all, these companies were well protected at all times. One of Herod's secrets was keeping his security people invisible. Intruders seldom had a clear target to focus on. Herod was a pioneer in state-of-the-art body protection and weaponry for his security personnel. All were well armed at all times. Herod's company became wildly successful using these simple and highly effective methods.

Matt wisely kept his father's business and, shortly after Herod's death, chose Arthur Piedmont to continue in his father's footsteps at SSS Inc.

Arthur had worked closely with Herod and they had worked as a team. Arthur's role initially had been procurement, and then he had become interested in organization and communication. One thing led to another, and the two men complemented one another, resulting in a stronger company that had continued to grow. It was because of Arthur, that Herod was able to spend more time with his son developing the new satellite security program. Space Security Watchers (SSW Inc) started, by launching satellites that now covered the Western US coast and included British Columbia. Canada. Other satellite sites included the upper US coastline from Massachusetts to Connecticut. At the moment, a new system had recently come into play; covering London, France and Germany. The Texas coastline was currently in development.

Their concept was to approach major warehousing located in the seaports of the US and Europe and sell 24/7 monitored surveillance, via high tech cameras. Each warehouse was equipped with large numbers of the high quality cameras. Video signals were relayed to satellites, and relayed to SSW Inc. monitoring offices. The plan was basically quite simple. When anything suspicious was observed in or around any given warehouse, the police were immediately contacted. The warehouse companies loved the concept, as did the various law enforcement agencies. Plus, space security was much more precise and constant than ground security. Warehouse theft on average had declined by thirty-nine percent, compared to the year previous. This was huge and translated to companies' increasing their profits, which more than offset the cost of surveillance.

The name; Space Security Watchers said it all. He inherited some of his early clientele from his dad's old business. Matt had an immediate success on his hands, and the new company was a hit. Sales rapidly rose into the stratosphere. Money was no longer an issue. Matt had never, in his wildest dreams, imagined having access to such wealth.

Now it was time for the next phase of his life: payback.

Their omelets arrived piping hot and both lapsed into silence as they ate the delicious breakfast. When they finished and were starting their second cup of coffee, Arthur spoke once more.

"How did you find the man who did it, and did you ever find out why?"

"I found out through the security tapes and from the new satellite imagery. In both instances we obtained a crystal clear picture of the guy who killed Dad. The video image was so clear that you could see the color of his eyes. His picture was then shown around the area and we managed to pinpoint him. I'll keep the name to myself for now, mostly for your protection.

"My father was killed because the company was doing too good a job. Thieves were being kept at bay with our security measures, so this particular individual chose to remove the head of the company, thinking that, without him, security would fall apart. The thieves waited for him to perform one of his nightly rounds in order to kill him. They'd have gotten away with it, if it weren't for the great work you and Dad had accomplished.

"As you know, he was shot through the head from behind, and died instantly. The man who murdered him were hiding in the shadows of a security shed, and when the security guard yelled, the assassin ran over to a waiting car and took off. Later, when things settled down a bit, I searched the warehouse to try and determine what they were looking for, but couldn't find anything suspicious. I then contacted a business associate who owned a guard dog business and they were able to sniff out drugs hidden in one of packing crates. We found a huge container of cocaine that was being stored short-term at the warehouse.

Somehow, the man I now have in my Explorer found out about the drugs and was trying to steal them from the warehouse. The authorities were contacted, and the people who had stored the drugs were apprehended. Unfortunately, lawyers found a few loopholes, resulting in only token sentences. The guy in my vehicle who killed Dad will remain our little secret. So, that clears up the why and who. This guy tonight was after you for about the same reason. This is the business he's in. He robs warehouses and seems to be well informed as to their contents. I'm taking this asshole somewhere where he won't bother anyone again! Reason being, I don't want the Asshole finding some asinine loophole and escape the justice he truly deserves!"

As though to ward off a follow-up question, Matt changed the subject.

"So, how are you liking your new position at Secure Security Sentries?"

"I love it Matt. It fits my lifestyle perfectly, and the staff is superb. I love the challenges, and it never gets boring. But I do miss Herod. He was such a gem to work for. The same goes for you as well, Matt."

Matt was glad to hear this, for he loved Arthur like a brother.

"Arthur, I'll be away for two or three weeks. Can you keep an eye on things for me?"

"Of course I will. Promise me that you'll keep in touch?"

"You can count on it."

The meeting was over. Both men got up, shook hands, and went their separate ways. Matt had much to accomplish in a short amount of time.

Chapter 2

Hello Again Asshole!

First things first. A supply of wood is stacked at the far end of the clearing in a lean-to.

You have enough food to do you for one month. Budget this food accordingly! Most is freeze dried. Simply read the instructions on the various packages, and you'll be fine. At the end of one month, another month's food supply will be delivered.

Appropriate clothing has been provided in a side room, and in another room you'll find your food supplies.

The river will take care of all your water needs. The river will also serve as your latrine.

You're sentenced to stay on this island for six months, unless you screw up or don't choose to obey the rules. If you choose to cooperate, you'll be allowed back into society with ONE stipulation. You'll get yourself a job, and become an upstanding citizen. But should you fuck up again, you'll be brought back here for the rest of your miserable life! You are here because you're an asshole and a bottom feeder. So use these six months to reflect on the rotten things you have done.

Should you decide to escape, you'll be brought back, and a year will be added to your sentence.

Soon, five other assholes—one or two at a time—will join you. Should you physically abuse each other in ANY way, ALL your food supplies will be cut in half. The second time this happens, food supplies will be cut in half again. If it happens a third time, ALL food supplies will be terminated, and you will all starve to death. Should it come to this, GOOD RIDDANCE!

One SAT phone is provided. It will always be kept in working condition. Use it ONLY for emergencies! If and when you phone, leave a message. You'll only have three calls during your stay on this island, so DO NOT phone unless you are in dire need! Your phone message will be returned, if it is extremely urgent.

To protect yourself once the other assholes arrive, be sure they too follow these instructions, and unless you want to be the one explaining them, I'd save this note.

Once again, you have all that you need to survive during your stay. You'll soon have company.

Jazz was stunned. *Who the fuck is doing this? Six months!* He wanted to scream in frustration. *I can't live like this!* He promised himself, he would find out who put him here and kill the son of a bitch!

Right now Jazz was tired and hungry. He began looking around for the promised food, which he located in a small separate pantry. It was all packaged inside vacuum foil type bags. Using his flashlight again, he read the instructions and found that hot water was to be added. *Shit! Now I have to go to the river to get water.* He put on a warm coat that was hung in a separate room. Outside, there was enough light to guide him. He grabbed a bucket and carefully walked down a rough path. It was still freezing, as he made his way to the edge of the river, and he was shocked at what he saw.

He could barely see land, and the river looked dangerously deep, fast and cold. Jazz didn't waste a lot of time looking. Scooping up water in the bucket, he quickly made his way back to the cabin. He opened a package of soup mix, emptied it into a pot, added water, and placed it on the stove. The water took forever to come to a boil. Jazz messed up in the directions, and the soup didn't look great, but he was famished, and right now, he could eat anything. After cramming down the disgusting mixture, he was at least sated. *What I wouldn't give for a Big Mac and fries!*

While seated at the table, he took the time to look around the large cabin. The cabin was made of heavy cedar-wood planks, held together by long metal spikes. The roof was covered by cedar-wood shakes. The cabin consisted of three rooms. The main room contained three double bunks, a stove in the center, a small counter containing cooking implements and a large plank table with two wood benches. Two shelves were loaded with varied types of books. One of the two separate rooms held food supplies and the other held various articles of clothing. Not far from the cabin, was a large pile of split cedar for the stove. Extra logs were stacked ready for cutting and splitting. The only implements consisted of an axe, two long handled spades and a two-handed lumber saw.

The island was teardrop in shape, with steep cliffs rising above the river on both sides. The upper and lower parts of the island had a gradual drop-off to the river's edge. The cabin was well hidden on the highest part of the island with a steep path descending down to the fast flowing water.

Jazz began to dredge up his past, which had started out bad and only gotten worse. His mother had been a prostitute, and his earliest memories consisted of hearing mysterious sounds coming from her bedroom. At times he either heard screams, moaning, raucous laughing or swearing. He had little to eat and often survived on crackers, peanut butter and baloney sandwiches. Milk had been a rarity. The only treat he could remember having, was a half-eaten hamburger and cold fries. Coke was the only drink in the fridge, for it was the favored mix for the rum his mother always drank and he could remember the beatings she administered whenever she caught him drinking any of it. The men who accompanied her to their small apartment were disgusting, dirty and foul-mouthed. He learned to keep himself invisible in his tiny room, while she was with her men friends, for he had frequently been fondled, beaten or cursed at by many of them.

By the age of twelve, he had had enough. One night, he put on his only coat, put two cans of coke into his pockets, and walked out, never to return. His first night was spent sleeping in an alley, and when he awoke, he found a large dog lying next to him for warmth. He shared a can of coke with the mongrel, and for the next few months, they became inseparable. An old couple, feeling sorry for their plight, let him and his dog sleep in their covered porch. He and the dog were fed twice a day, if Jazz would perform chores around their home. This lasted only a week, and he was told to leave after they caught him eating a freshly baked apple pie, which had been cooling on the porch windowsill. That pie had been the best food he had ever eaten! He continued to wander the streets, stole food or went through garbage cans to survive.

A few weeks later, a gang of kids dragged him into an alley and badly beat him and his dog. One of them had slashed his arm with a knife. They gave him a few good kicks for good measure and left him unconscious and bleeding from the knife wound.

A kind passerby stopped and took him to a service station to clean him up, bandage his arm and gave him two dollars so he could feed himself and his dog. And so it went. Eventually, his dog was run over by a passing motorist who didn't even bother to stop. That dog was the only thing he had ever loved. Shortly after, he was caught stealing food from a corner deli store and the authorities had placed him in a foster home. Jazz ran away after continued beatings and sexual abuse.

When he was sixteen, he was put in juvenile detention for the attempted robbery of a service station. It was there he learned about the drug world. By the time he was released, he had made a few connections and managed to survive quite well in the world of drugs. He also acquired a taste for music and from then on, was always seen listening to music of all forms, until he finally settled on the jazz world and couldn't get enough of it. Up to that point, he had gone by the name of Hogue. His cohorts nicknamed him Jazz. He liked the sound of the nickname and from then on, he became known as Jazz Hogue.

He enjoyed beating on seniors and robbing them, and his world turned ever more violent as he progressed upwards in the drug world. It eventually became necessary to kill occasionally whenever his gang-members betrayed him, or losers who failed to pay him for supplying them with drugs. He became bitter as time went by, because both women and men shunned him due to his temper and cruelty. He was not handsome, had close-set eyes and a long broken nose. The only people who stuck around him were those that were paid. He was close to no one.

To help pass the time, Jazz kept busy by stocking the cabin with wood, carrying water from the river, familiarized himself with the contents of the cabin, reviewed some of the books which were in plentiful supply and explored the island. He soon determined that escape did indeed prove an impossible task. His final chore was to make himself another disgusting meal from one of the packages. He vowed to himself that he would soon teach himself how to cook.

Jazz was tired beyond belief. He drank some water, unrolled one of the sleeping bags on a lower bunk, and lay there waiting for sleep to come. Jazz Hogue was still pissed! *What the fuck will happen tomorrow?* He was scared, lonely and missed his jazz music. He finally rolled over and descended into a troubled sleep.

Outside, the wind began to blow, and a heavy snow started to fall. Darkness descended. It was the blackest of nights.

Chapter 3

Harry Blankford, known as the Bear of Seattle, woke up with a sore arm and neck. He was hungry and unbearably cold and in a foul temper. Morning was starting to break. He couldn't remember ever being so groggy and fuzzy headed. He stood up slowly and looked around, trying to orient himself. He was wearing hiking boots --- where the fuck did those come from? Straight ahead, at eye level, he could see a note pinned to a tree, by a small knife.

Hello Asshole!

How does it feel to be on the receiving end for a change?
Read this carefully...

—

Jazz Hogue had just jumped back into his sleeping bag after firing up the cold stove. He was waiting for the coffee to perk in an ancient metal coffeepot. He had finally learned how to make a fairly decent cup of coffee after three days of frustrating effort. Prior to being here, he had never cooked anything for himself in his life. He was looking at the calendar on the wall and the three Xs, which he had begun marking, in order to keep track of his days spent on the island.

So far, his simple routine was to relieve himself in the river—where he had twice lost his balance and almost fell in—then carry a fresh pail of water back up to the cabin, bring in a day's worth of wood, and then hunker down inside the warm cabin. His time was spent preparing his next meal and reading one of the many books on a shelf over the table. Thank God he had learned how to read in juvie. Books included: cooking, medical, how to survive in the wild, a Bible, positive living, as well as a host of other crap. *Jesus, who read books like this?* At least he learned a little about cooking, which he sorely needed. Things were boring and he feared he would lose his mind long before his six months were up. The silence, loneliness and stress were really starting to get to him.

As he lay inside his cozy sleeping bag, contemplating the rest of his day, the door to the cabin was suddenly kicked open by a crazy looking bastard, who charged over to him and dragged him to his feet, holding a knife to his throat. The man was full of rage.

"Either you tell me why I'm here, or I will fuckin' kill you!"

Jazz could already feel blood trickling down his throat from the small stab wound and was terrified.

"We're not to hurt each other," he pleaded, "or we'll starve to death! Just read the instructions on the table. I'm a prisoner too!"

The crazy bastard took the knife from Jazz's throat and threw him to the floor.

"Don't you move, you piece of shit!"

The man walked over to the table and read the note. When he was finished reading he turned back to Jazz, still furious.

"How the fuck did we get here?"

"I have no fucking clue," said Jazz. "I've been wondering the same thing. I've been here three days already." *Thank God this asshole is starting to calm down,* he thought, cowering on the floor. *How the fuck am I going to live with this madman for six months?*

The newcomer took a deep breath.

"We have to get off this fuckin' island and quick."

"There's no way to do it," Jazz said. "But if we did and they caught us again, we'd be returned and, well, you read the note. I don't have any answers."

Calm finally prevailed, and before they started figuring the next step, poured themselves a cup of the now steaming coffee. After five minutes of silence, Bear introduced himself and asked Jazz where he was from before being brought here. They were both surprised they came from the same city. Bear was a fearsome looking individual, and when he talked, Jazz carefully listened.

"First of all," Bear said, "if we were to escape, how would they find us again? Second of all, if we were to injure one another, how would they fuckin' know? Something is not adding up."

"How about we wait for the next food delivery, thirty days from now, and ambush the son of a bitch who delivers them?"

"That's one idea," Bear said. "Now let's see what else we can come up with. But before we do, I'm starving, how about some fuckin' food!"

"I'm just starting to get the hang of cooking. Three days ago, when I got here, I'd never cooked anything in my life, so I'm still not great at it." Jazz said.

"I'll eat anything at this point, so get on with it!"

Jazz poured water into the only pot and waited for it to start boiling, then added oatmeal. When it was ready, he filled two metal bowls and brought them to the table. They ate in silence.

Tastes like shit, Bear thought, but realized that there was no point mentioning it. *I couldn't do much better; besides, better to have this dipshit do most of the work.*

"How's about you going to get my supplies?" he said. "I'm still fuckin' frozen from waking up on the goddamn cold ground."

Jazz obliged, wary of his new cabin-mate and glad for the break. He dressed for the cold and trudged to the other end of the island to begin the task. The new supplies matched those left for him a few days prior, including an extra windup flashlight.

After three trips and an hour's work, Jazz completed the task and they began to plot their escape.

Twenty-two miles overhead, a satellite system was relaying all they were saying and doing, via hidden cameras in the cabin ceiling, feeding the video to a nearby satellite dish and finally to a computer monitor in Matt's hunting lodge. The information being received was astounding; it was like watching a movie with perfect sound. Sounds outside the cabin were also picked up and relayed by well-placed sound enhancers, placed strategically throughout the island, thus enabling the monitoring devices to listen in on virtually any conversation.

The failsafe to all this was a transmitter located inside the heels of the captives hiking boots. The boots had been fitted to their feet during their unconscious state—this transmitter could locate their position, via GPS, to within a few feet, anywhere in the world, as long as they were wearing the boots.

Chapter 4

Jeff Harrigan was monitoring the island from Matt's hunting lodge. He was fascinated with the equipment he had been given in order to accomplish his assignment. The first computer showed him what was happening 24/7 inside the cabin, while the second computer monitored the island, utilizing various well-hidden cameras (CCTV) and a sophisticated sound system. The third monitored the transmitters imbedded inside each man's hiking boots, precisely positioning and identifying each man. The latter method utilizes a GPS system and is accurate to a few feet.

At this moment, he was monitoring their current conversation and Bear was starting to lose his temper once again and growing increasingly frustrated by their plight. So far, the rules were being followed, although Jazz was being cowed into doing most of the work. He was attempting to do all of the food preparation. Bear was trying to form an escape plan, but as yet, nothing was coming together.

At one point Bear left the cabin, slammed the door behind him, and walked the area in order to survey what they were up against. Bear could see the challenge of escape was thwarted by the ferocity of the fast flowing river. Land was almost invisible. He could see that escape was virtually impossible. The only plan, so far, was to capture the supply vessel due to deliver their supplies in a month. It was cold, windy and the sky was slightly overcast. He slowly returned to the warmth of the cabin.

Jeff's SAT phone rang and Matt Chambers came on the line.

"How are our guests liking their new quarters?"

"As we expected, tempers are raw. They're stressed, confused and frustrated."

"True justice is measured in satisfaction, isn't it?" said Matt.

"I've been thinking along those lines too. There's something about these two that fascinates me."

"What exactly?"

"Both appear to think about the same, neither will confide in the other, and seem to have similar backgrounds. They did admit to each other that they were from Seattle though."

"Great observations, Jeff. I think you'll find the future occupants will prove more interesting still. How is all the equipment working"?

"Couldn't be better," he said. "The images are clear as a bell, and I swear to God, their voices sound as clear as our phone conversation. The transmitters inside the hiking boots are sheer genius!"

"The foot-ware is something of an experiment for the company. Our new product development division has come up with a GPS transmitting device that is permanently sealed inside the heels of hiking boots, shoes or runners. A new membrane we've developed constantly recharges the lithium batteries that run the transmitter. When the foot ware is worn outside, the membrane of the boot acts as a kind of solar panel and recharges the batteries. We're keeping this division completely secret for now. Only a few people in our company are wearing them, on an experimental basis. The boot itself not only looks good; but also is also warm and quite comfortable. We have a good number of all sizes, which makes it easy to fit anyone's foot. They are perfectly suited to our island prisoners."

"Are you happy with the assignment so far, Jeff?"

"There's nowhere else I'd rather be, Matt. But you already know that! I have everything I need. Just keep those supplies rolling in. I can't begin to tell you how pleasing it is to be part of this. It's better than any movie I've ever seen. By the way, when can I expect the next four visitors?"

Matt's reply was typically vague.

"It'll happen soon. Can you touch base with me about this time every day?"

"Noonish every day? I can do that," Jeff said.

"Great! I'll talk to you tomorrow then."

"Sounds good, Matt. And thank you for all you've done for me."

Jeff was working from Matt's hunting lodge, about a half hour's drive to the river's edge. From there, the island was barely discernable. He was comfortable being in this isolated spot, for he had grown tired of past cruelty and the ineptness of man. It had happened eighteen months ago. He had been working a late shift with the security firm owned by Matt Chambers and had received a phone call from the monitoring company indicating that his home security had been breeched. Jeff had jumped into his car and raced to his home and found it in shambles. Police and firemen were everywhere and barriers had been set up to keep traffic and people away. He had to fight the crowds to get through and had to show identification to get past the police.

Bullet holes, wreckage and blood were everywhere. Jeff was in a rage and demanded to speak to the officer in charge. He was told that, if he would calm down, they would grant his request. The lieutenant in charge spoke to him and absolutely forbade him to enter his home, as he would contaminate the crime scene.

Jeff was informed briefly about what had taken place. His wife had been murdered and his son and daughter killed by machine gun fire. That's when he had lost it, vomited in some nearby shrubbery, broke down and cried like a baby. The lieutenant put his hand on Jeff's shoulder until he recovered.

He learned later that his house had been mistakenly targeted by a local drug cartel trying to recover stolen drug money. The police were of little help, as they had little to go on. Drug business in Seattle was rampant and Jeff was assured that he'd be contacted as soon as they had any viable leads.

The only person that Jeff thought to call at that point had been Matt Chambers. Within the half hour, Matt arrived and took him straight to his own home. Matt had a settling effect on him and listened patiently until he managed to calm down. Jeff had been a mess and didn't have a clue what to do next. Matt sat in a separate lounger while his wife, Kirsten, sat with Jeff and held his hand. Jeff finally started to relax and was put to bed in one of the spare rooms. He slept only a little and nightmares of his family being killed haunted him through the morning hours.

Jeff Harrigan was one of Matt's best security people. He was ex-army intelligence and had proven his loyalty to Matt's company countless times. His suggestions on how to improve security and general communications far exceeded what he was being paid. Jeff would not be let down.

Matt's next step was to contact his investigators to determine who was responsible for this tragic affair. The reward he very privately offered was a hundred thousand dollars, paid on the condition that any information would be for his ears only. Suffice it to say that, within the month, the man responsible was caught and delivered to one of Matt's warehouses, located on Seattle's Southside.

Jazz Hogue was a dangerous man who had faced his share of adversity, but it only took the breaking of one finger to convince the man to come clean. He sang like a bird and told Matt and his two investigators everything in great detail. They knew they had the ringleader. A while later, they administered a drug that would render him unconscious for a long time. His broken finger was partially repaired with a makeshift splint.

Matt didn't immediately share with Jeff any information pertaining to his findings, but did approach him with a lucrative opportunity that would perhaps allow Jeff to start making a difference in the world. The plan was laid out, and Jeff was more than interested. He also wanted to drop out of society for a while during his grieving process. Matt's proposal was ideal for Jeff. It would also help him adjust to his loss and give him a worthwhile challenge on which to concentrate.

The site where this would all happen was already in place. The location was Matt's remote hunting lodge located in the northern wilds of British Columbia. A private airstrip was located close by. The lodge was difficult to find and an ideal place for his purposes. Another mission in Matt's life was about to come into being.

Chapter 5

In the Southern United States, he was the undisputed king of the of the underworld drug trade. His method of achieving success was a simple one: Frank Herrick killed off his competition. Within his organization was a group of five mercenaries whose sole mission was to kill anyone who attempted to get in Frank's way. The victims in every case were brutalized before being murdered, in order to send out a clear signal of the consequences of tampering with Frank Herrick's empire. Everyone killed was put on display. In one instance a headless victim was hung by his heels from a bridge—his head and testicles were located inside a sack tied to his belt. In another instance, a man was found buried in cement with only his head showing. He had been alive when they put him there, and they waited for the cement to harden before departing. The message was clear, and the competition stayed away in droves!

His business location was in the south district of Los Angeles, and his multi-million dollar mansion was located in Bel Air. The two-story mansion was situated on twenty acres of prime real estate, surrounded by a ten-foot high brick fence. A remote control sliding metal fence provided sole access to the property. His five mercenaries lived with him in elaborate quarters in the basement of the mansion. When he and his men were absent from the property, two well-armed guards took their place with orders to kill anyone who tried to access the property. Three servants were employed to take care of their every need. Frank Herrick had never married. No woman could bear up to his cruel ways.

He surrounded himself with the best lawyers in California, and law enforcement agencies seldom troubled Merrick or his henchmen. He was a very careful man who didn't hesitate offering huge bribes to people in power. A few of the uncooperative power people, who chose not to cooperate, simply disappeared!

Herrick's latest venture was to have his drug lab produce a unique drug that couldn't be duplicated. The drug was coined "Crack'r Jack" and was aimed at capturing the ever lucrative schools for the rich. Age was no object. The drug was so successful that it shortly made its way to the Northern States. Any kid who tried it loved the effect and was soon badly hooked. There was only one problem. The only side effect was death—should the drug be taken within an hour of the previous hit.

This was happening with alarming regularity, and one of the children who died while using Crack'r Jack happened to be a good friend of nine-year old Sam Chambers. Sam had found his friend during recess, unconscious beside a fence located behind his school. The boy was in a bad way, and hardly breathing. Sam called for help, and an ambulance was dispatched to the school and by the time it arrived, the boy was pronounced dead. Sam was heartbroken, and as his friend was taken away, he simply sat on the ground and wept.

His bodyguard, whose job assignment was to safely convey his employer's children to and from school, finally located Sam. The bodyguard's name was Barney Satch, and he quickly found out what had happened and immediately alerted his boss, Matt Chambers. Barney lifted Sam and carried him inside the school, proceeded to security and had them find Sam's sister, Mia. He then drove them home. Mia held Sam's hand the whole way. By the time the children were brought home from school, their parents were there to greet them. Sam looked so vulnerable and heartbroken. His parent's took the children into the house and tried to console Sam. Mia sat beside him and continued to hold his hand.

Later, when the children were tucked into bed, Matt would again call in his investigators to discreetly find out exactly what were the circumstances that led up to the death of Sam's friend.

It took two months to find where the drug originated. Matt was informed about the Crack'r Jack that caused the young boy's death and the lab from which it came. This time, Matt decided to personally handle the situation.

Matt made some calls on his secure SAT phone.

Frank Herrick, in the meantime, was holidaying in his chateau in southern France. The reason he chose France was that he liked the beauty of the region and he particularly liked the high-class Parisian whores. He would usually pick them up from only the best of Paris hotels and entice them to accompany him to his chateau. They always loved to ride in his luxurious Rolls Royce Phantom. One of these prostitutes was with him on the second night of his stay and after a sumptuous dinner, prepared by his chef, they retired to his bedroom. The first thing he did was to knock out the girl, using his fists. He then handcuffed her from behind and taped her mouth shut. When she regained consciousness, he got himself worked up by beating her some more and then took his time sodomizing and raping her throughout the night. A few hours later he dumped her unceremoniously into the trunk of his Rolls, drove back towards Paris and, on a side road, removed the handcuffs, ripped the tape from her mouth, once more knocked her out and then rolled her into a ditch. He leisurely drove back to his Chateau to enjoy a marvelous nights' sleep.

He got off on cruelty. At an early age, he had beaten both his parents to death with a baseball bat in retaliation for their varied cruelties on him. He frequently took pleasure from this memory.

Chapter 6

For the first day in weeks, Nina Sparrow was taking time off to relax. She was lying down on her comfortable lounger, letting the early morning sun do its work on her skin. It was the most relaxing activity (inactivity) for her. The computer work of the prior evening had been particularly stressful and she needed to unwind. Her venture on the computer had been tough, but at the conclusion, she had nailed another crooked organization. It was always a high for her and always would be. *They would be squirming badly by now!*

While she was contemplating all this, her peaceful sojourn came to an end, when her special SAT phone rang. She knew it was Matt Chambers because he had given it to her in order to keep their conversations completely private. Nina loved his phone calls because they were always challenging, interesting and lucrative. He needed her computer acumen, as she could hack her way into anything. She did not come cheap, but price was no object. She was shrewd and knew how to both enter and back out of any computer without leaving any trace. She had yet to let Matt down. He had retained her services in the past for security checks for a few of his clients.

As usual, she became instantly interested in his latest venture. Matt proposed that, prior to travelling to Las Angeles, in two days, she would have some computer work to perform. It would be something new and challenging and she was asked to actively participate as well! She agreed to his proposal and would accompany him in the company's Learjet to LA. But the two days prior to departure, her first assignment was to find out all she could about Frank Herrick—using any means at her disposal. Price was no object. When he rang off, Nina had a sudden adrenalin rush, jumped up and immediately set to work.

Nina had always been a rebel. She questioned everything. At an early age, she could remember overhearing her parents speak on the subject of corporate bribery and the people who were affected. Nina researched these organizations using her computer but could penetrate only so far. And then one of her friends introduced her to an underground hacker who had a reputation for performing serious penetration on a host of corporations. He and Nina made an immediate connection and he agreed to show her the ropes.

Her first task was to demonstrate her computer talents on a local bank. The hacker watched her as she made her keystrokes, and then asked her to reverse exactly the same way she had gone in. After a few tries she succeeded and was told that backing out was as important as going in, and he emphasized NOT to leave any tracks. She was shown a gizmo that prevented hackers from being traced. She was astounded at the ease with which he cracked a company's security. The device he used was invented and perfected by him.

She proved to be a quick study and was asked to do a simple corporate penetration, as a test. She amazed him by easily accessing the site but needed help backing out. He had her repeat the procedure until she could do it rapidly and safely. He then had her enter and crack the company's security. It took her a while before gaining access, under his watchful eye. The next assignment was to penetrate three major sites, repeating the same procedure.

She was a natural, and during the weeks that followed, she learned everything there was to learn. Her final lesson was never to transfer any funds, as this was too easy to track and charges would certainly be laid.

Nina was told to keep in close touch with him, because of the many changes constantly being made in the computer world. She was provided with a few pieces of the equipment he invented, and she promised to pay him for it when she came up with the money.

Now she was equipped to start making a few changes that she had always had been wanting to make. She experimented in her room one night while her parents were out for the evening. She accessed one of her corporate targets and gained access to their email account. After two hours of looking, she downloaded some pretty serious incriminating information and downloaded the information to a memory stick.

The next day she visited an Internet cafe and sent contents to the local newspaper. The results proved quite satisfactory. Three people were arrested as a result and charged with bribery, but, although they were heavily fined, jail time was averted. She found out later that the attending judge was told not to hand out any jail time, due to the overcrowding. Nina was furious but found herself powerless to do anything about it. She vowed to herself that she would never stop trying to catch the frauds of the world. She continued to make progress but that progress was slow and the results infuriating.

The only computer site she failed to access was Space Security Watchers. The public information she found on them intrigued her, and she decided to pay the company a visit. Nina arrived early one morning and simply sat in the lobby to observe the type of people that were employed by the company. Thirty minutes later, a man stopped and asked her if he could help her. She decided that honesty was the best policy and simply replied that the company intrigued her and that she had dropped by to check it out.

The man introduced himself as Matt Chambers, the owner of the company and asked her if she would like a short tour. She was thrilled and they spent the next two hours touring. She asked Matt a thousand questions. Surprisingly, she found herself confiding that her ambition was to bring some justice to the world by exposing those people in positions of power that brought misery to the less fortunate. Matt happened to be looking for her type of expertise at the time and decided to retain her services on a freelance bases. The business chemistry between them blossomed.

—

It had been a productive day, and Barney Satch had just picked up Matt from his office. Matt noticed that Barney was quieter than usual during the drive home. Barney was his personal driver and in charge of the security of his family.

"Barney, are you happy with our justice system?"

Barney was surprised by the question and took longer to answer the question than Matt expected. In fact, Barney pulled over before answering. He turned, then, to face Matt.

"My sister is presently married to a complete asshole. He often beats on her and takes pleasure in it. She won't leave him because he's threatened to hurt their child, when he finds them again. I'm very close to her, and I've threatened him to stop with the cruelty or else. He simply replies that, should I interfere, he will call the police and have me charged. I did go to the police, and all they said, was to inform them should these beatings persist. They pointed out that the complaint would have to come from my sister. Now they have me on file, because I reported the complaint and that'll only make it easier for them to charge me should I act on my threat."

Matt thought before answering,

"What if she leaves him and goes into hiding?"

"She won't," he said. "He has mob connections. He would find her and her son and…"

Barney stopped talking for a minute, as he was starting to lose it.

"Is there anything that I can do to help?"

Barney looked lost. "Not much *can* be done, Matt. But I really appreciate you asking."

He then pulled back into the traffic, and they continued the drive home. Before Matt emerged from the car, he asked Barney the names of his sister and her husband and their address—he had all this on file of course, but he wanted Barney to know he was interested. Barney's sister's name was Sara, and her husband was Chester Bennett.

"Barney, would it be okay if I made some discreet inquiries?"

"About Chester? Be my guest; just be *sure* they're discreet Matt. I don't want anything coming back on me, Sara or her son."

"You have my word," Matt said as he emerged from the car.

Matt had one more call to make. He contacted his investigating team and had them find out more about Chester Bennett's activities and also have him watched 24/7.

Chapter 7

Nina Sparrow was picked up by Barney early Saturday morning to join Matt, who was already at the airport, briefing his pilot regarding the itinerary for the next week.

Nina had never met Barney before, but became quite intrigued by him. Barney was a good- looking man. He was tall, had blue eyes, a ready smile and a great disposition. In order to get him to talk, she began by barraging him with questions. Where was he from? Did he have family? Was he married? How long had he worked for Matt? Did he find his work interesting?

Barney easily opened up to her, which was unusual for him; he was usually quiet and pensive by nature. His response to Nina about Matt was very open and positive, because he had a huge respect for his employer and was openly encouraged to talk about his background and his beliefs. He felt Matt cared for people and tried to make a difference in their lives. Matt also welcomed suggestions and always provided follow-up to all suggestions. Nina liked what she was hearing about Matt. She also liked working for Matt, for the same reasons.

When they arrived at the airport, Barney very shyly asked her if he could take her to lunch on her return trip. Nina was thrilled with his request and immediately accepted the invitation, which was unusual for her—she had a tendency to distance herself from relationships due to the nature of her work.

Barney couldn't wait for her to return. He was fascinated with her; she seldom talked about herself but only about him. Right now, he found that he was very curious to find out more about her. She was barely five feet tall and looked to be in great shape. She was very cute, had a great figure and was intelligent to boot! When they arrived at Seattle-Tacoma International, Nina politely thanked him for the ride, and, before departing, mentioned how much she was looking forwarding seeing him again.

Barney Satch had been introduced to Herod Chambers after he had completed two stints with the US Marines. His final two years had been spent as a Navy Seal, specializing in demolition and infiltration. He served in Afghanistan during his final year and thankfully left the service without injury. Barney was a firm believer that Afghanistan was a waste of time, money and young lives. The number of wounded and maimed still haunted him. He felt that bad leaders in power throughout history were the cause of too many casualties and untold world debt. As a result of war, the United States national debt was skyrocketing, the country was being badly neglected and corruption was rampant. The government was badly at odds with itself, and too many companies that benefitted from war had grown rich because of it. Consequently, lobbying for war was crucial to their survival. Barney was glad to be finally out of it.

He had applied with Secure Security Sentries and within the week, he was employed on a full time bases. Herod Chambers had only hired men of great ability and integrity. Training and communication were stressed, and all employees were encouraged to think on their feet. Suggestions were welcomed and rewarded. Herod had always treated him like an equal, and Barney became fiercely loyal to him. On the night that Herod Chambers had been murdered, Barney had been on duty at the warehouse where the tragedy had occurred. He had blamed himself ever since. If only he could have reacted faster! He had observed Herod as he drove up to the warehouse, while doing his usual rounds of checking on his men, and as he emerged from his car, a man had stepped out from behind a building and shot him in back of the head. Barney had yelled at the man to stop and ran to catch him, but the murderer had jumped into a car, hidden in shadows and managed to escape. Barney immediately called 911. Then he called Secure Security Sentries.

The ambulance and police arrived within minutes, but Herod was pronounced dead. Matt and the security team arrived as the ambulance was driving off. Matt was so stunned, he could hardly function, but he still had enough sense to recognize Barney's emotional strain, and asked to meet with him the following day.

Matt had quickly recognized that increased security was becoming more important to his family and business. When they met the following day, Matt had asked Barney if he was interested in watching over his family. Barney welcomed the change and his immediate priority was to provide the security for Matt's wife and children.

Nina made her way through security and found Matt, who was waiting for her, prior to boarding.

"How was your ride to the airport?"

"I enjoyed the trip and being picked up by such a handsome chauffeur."

Matt simply smiled and suggested boarding his Learjet, as they had just received clearance to start taxiing. The copilot relieved Nina of her overnight bag, while Matt offered to take her briefcase. The occupants of the plane consisted of Matt, Nina, Matt's aide; Ryan O'Hare, the pilot and copilot.

The plane's interior was beautiful, and the décor was exquisite. It had ten comfortable spacious seats. Matt and Nina belted themselves in, facing each other, separated by a handsome, round oak table. The plane started to taxi down the runway, and was quickly airborne. Ryan asked them what they preferred for refreshments. Both chose a glass of Cabernet Sauvignon, but deferred to a later lunch, and, without preamble, proceeded to discuss their itinerary.

Nina opened her briefcase and took out a maroon folder, which she referred to during the ensuing conversation. It was the information about what she had been able to put together pertaining to Frank Herrick. Most of her report was garnered from hacking into Herrick's company computer. She was able to determine that a lot of funds were transferred from a Los Angeles banking firm to a bank in the Caymans. His business was located in the Movat Office Tower, located just north of Santa Monica Freeway on Washington Boulevard. The name of his company was Kings Quick

Delivery. He was presently on holiday in his Chateau near Paris, accompanied by five men and was due to return to LA Monday evening. She handed Matt the addresses of his Chateau in Paris and his LA Bel Air home address.

Matt also opened a dossier, which contained information gathered from his LA investigators. He handed it to her. It read; Frank Herrick is well known to us. All of his money is derived from the drugs he has made from his own laboratories in LA. His latest and most lucrative drug is known as Crack'r Jack and his lab has recently expanded, in order to keep up with the demand. It is not known how he launders his money before sending it out of the country. He is constantly accompanied by five of the most ruthless thugs imaginable. They have "eliminated" a lot of people. "Enclosed, is a picture of him with three of his men, taken only days ago as he was emerging from The Ritz-Carlton hotel in LA. He is not a nice person. He is tall, good looking, physically fit, shrewd, completely ruthless, sadistic and cruel. He is also virtually untouchable. Officials and various governmental agencies are afraid to go near him. His cover company goes by the name of Kings Quick Delivery located in the Movat Office Tower, also in LA. He operates a fleet of trucks and most are used for legit delivery, but a few are used for moving his drugs. He has devised a method of packing these drugs in such a way as to completely avoid detection by dogs or mechanical means. Note: We strongly advise that you to be extremely careful in dealing with him. He and his men are DANGEROUS! Herrick owns three luxury cars in LA and a Rolls Royce Phantom at his Paris Chateau. His group of five mercenaries constantly guards him --- End of report.

When she finished reading the presentation, Matt laid out his plan for LA.

A lunch break was taken and they enjoyed a delicious salad and fresh rolls, served once more by Ryan O'Hare. Matt then excused himself make a phone call.

The call was to an ex army buddy now living in Paris, who presently went by the name of Fred Mills. During their stint in the army, Fred's specialty had been in demolition. Fred was presently in the business of supplying security personnel to visiting dignitaries who stayed at various

French hotels. Matt asked him if he was interested in some short-term employment? Fred indicated that he was indeed available. Matt laid out his plan. Frank Herrick's chateau and Rolls were to be located and his activities closely monitored. Matt read him the report that Nina had just reviewed and advised Fred to be very careful.

The next part of the plan was to wait until Herrick was on his way to the airport Monday evening, prior to rigging explosives, designed in such a way as to completely obliterate his Chateau and car. A phone signal performed by Matt Chambers would serve to detonate both the chateau and the Rolls simultaneously. Fred was to call Matt when all the explosives were in place, to report Herrick's activities and to ensure his exact departure time. Matt's instructions were explicit in ensuring that no one was to be killed inside the chateau, at the time of the explosion.

Chapter 8

The approach to Los Angeles International was slightly delayed, and after a smooth landing, they taxied to the Space Security Watchers' private hangar. The evening was clear and cool. Their gear was offloaded into a nondescript black Chrysler rental, parked beside the hangar. Matt, Nina and Ryan climbed into the van and drove from the airport.

First stop on their agenda was Frank Herrick's mansion in Bel Air. They arrived a little after ten in the evening and were confronted by a large estate, surrounded by high brick walls and an intimidating, secured metal gate. They drove past the estate and parked a few blocks away, and before exiting the van, Matt left instructions that he would call Nina and Ryan on his SAT phone, to let them know when it was ok to join him. Matt was well camouflaged for night work. His pockets were filled with items needed for his immediate mission—he wanted no unnecessary baggage. He disappeared around the south fence, and was soon in his element. He carefully moved to the rear of the property and silently scaled the high brick fence, dropped to his stomach behind some shrubbery and stealthily surveyed the area, using a compact night vision scope.

Matt spotted only one guard—whom he rapidly dispatched with a tranquilizer dart to the neck. The guard fell to the ground without emitting a sound. The unconscious guard was dragged to a nearby group of trees. Matt then proceeded to the front door and simply rang the front doorbell and ran back to where the first guard was now hidden. After a five-minute wait, a second guard cautiously made his way from the back of the house. He was wearing a black T-shirt, black pants and dark runners.

When he ventured near Matt's hiding place, Matt hit him squarely in his chest with another dart. Guard number two gasped and fell to the ground.

Using the keys from the first guard's pocket, he quickly let himself into the mansion. Once inside, he discovered a deactivated house alarm. The guards had been careless and probably bored in their lonely duties. He quickly scouted the rest of the mansion—the only sign of any recent habitation was a coffee machine in the kitchen, containing freshly made coffee and a stack of unwashed dishes. No other people were present.

The switch that controlled the front gate was located and the gate was opened. Matt phoned Ryan to drive in and join him. Nina and Ryan brought in their gear and the three began searching the mansion. Nina made the first major discovery in the upper master bedroom closet. She discovered a large safe cleverly hidden behind a sliding panel.

Matt attached a gizmo to the safe and activated it. A screen showing three zeros appeared and he began to slowly work the safe's dial, first one way and then the other. Numbers soon appeared on the electronic gizmo's readout. It took Matt only minutes to find the correct combination. The door to the safe was swung open. The contents revealed; stacks of cash, a laptop and eight packages of cocaine. They also found a ring of keys, an assortment of car key fobs, a pass card, and a small notebook containing phone numbers, bank account information and a series of what looked to be codes of some sort. The safe was left open and empty.

Matt and Ryan stuffed the safe contents into two empty duffel bags. Nothing else of interest was found in the mansion.

While Nina carried the filled duffel bags to the panel truck, Matt and Ryan quickly began placing explosives throughout the house and garage. Wires from all the charges were connected to a receiver, which would be set off later by dialing a number on Matt's SAT phone.

Time to lock up and leave. Matt and Ryan reopened the gate and transported the unconscious guards into the van. Ryan backed the truck outside the gate and it automatically closed behind them.

Herrick's office building was their next stop. They managed to find Movat Office Tower a little after one a.m., and again, Matt scouted the building. The doors were doubly locked, and all the glass appeared to be shatter resistant. Not an easy building to enter. Nina produced the keys from Herrick's safe, and after only two tries, they were in. The elevator carried them up to the King's Quick Delivery penthouse office but discovered the door could not be opened unless a security card was inserted into a slot located on a panel beside of the elevator door. They used the pass card taken from the mansion, and, upon insertion, the door opened. Matt and Ryan swept the floor for other security but found everything clear.

Herrick's glass desk was located in the exact center of his office, with only a phone, a pad of paper and a pen on its surface. A bar area and three oak filing cabinets lined the left wall and to the right, a bank of windows overlooked the parking lot far below. There had to be a computer somewhere, and after a ten-minute search, they located a huge safe concealed behind a cleverly constructed sliding panel. Matt repeated the same procedure using the electronic gizmo and, and a few minutes later, managed to open it. The safe was laden with neatly bundled stacks of fifty and hundred dollar bills, two more laptops, three ledgers and half a dozen handguns. Drugs were not present. They loaded everything into three duffel bags and quickly exited the building, leaving both the safe and panel wide open. The exterior doors were relocked as they left the premises.

The final stop was Frank Herrick's drug lab. The address had been found inside Herrick's notebook. On the way there, they stopped at a small park and deposited the still-sleeping guards handcuffed to a park bench and continued to their destination. The lab was located on the premises of Atlantic Dry Cleaning. The building was freestanding, with two parking lots, one located in front and the other behind the building. Thick metal bars protected the doors and windows. Matt again quickly gained entry using the same ring of keys obtained from the mansion, and the three entered, each carrying a heavy duffel bag. They proceeded through the premises and encountered a heavy metal door protected by a numbered keyboard. Nina again found various codes from the notebook and after three tries, the door swung silently open.

The lab was elaborately set up with state of the art drug-making equipment. This was where Crack'r Jack was being manufactured, confirmed by one of the ledgers found in Herrick's penthouse office. A small safe was located and opened by Matt. It contained drug formulas and addresses of the employees. This was placed on one of the counters. Explosives were placed throughout the lab and they repeated the same explosive layout they had used at the mansion. They relocked both doors and exited the building. The streets were void of cars and people.

They drove to a Holiday Inn, checked in, and used the outside entrance to carry in all the duffel bags into the two-bedroom suite. Nina was assigned one bedroom, while the other was for Matt and Ryan. The exhausted trio were asleep in minutes.

The smell of coffee greeted Matt and Ryan eight hours later. Nina had risen early in order to start what she was best at. She had also showered and fetched a large pot of coffee from the concierge. They drank the welcome brew and planned their day. Breakfast was ordered, and while it was on its way, Frank and Ryan took turns shaving and showering. By now, breakfast had arrived, and they feasted on bacon and eggs, waffles and toast.

They started the next phase of their plan.

Nina had already hacked into Frank Herrick's laptops. Her first duty was to locate his Cayman bank account, using the passwords gleaned from the evening's activities. The Cayman account held over two billion US dollars. Matt had Nina evenly transferred funds to a ghost account then transferred the funds to fifteen separate US charity organizations, all donated by the benevolence of Frank Herrick. She would repeat the procedure for Herrick's LA account. While she was doing all this, Matt and Ryan counted the money from the duffel bags they had taken from the safe. The count was over three million dollars.

Next, all credit card accounts were identified and would be cancelled while Frank Herrick and his men were in midair and on their way home.

They finished by five p.m. Sunday, dressed, and went out for a well-deserved dinner, retiring early, for it had been another exhausting day.

The call came at five a.m. Monday morning. Fred Mills was reporting in. It was two p.m. Monday in Paris. Fred gave Matt his verbal report.

"They've just boarded the plane. When they left the Chateau, I stayed behind with one of my men, and the explosives are now set. We sedated the servants while they were sleeping and took them with us when we left. The cell number you gave me will trigger the charges when you make the call. Let the phone ring three times, and you'll hear a squealing sound, which will indicate that it has happened. He added: This Herrick is a real prick. A couple of days ago when we had him under surveillance around four in the morning, he emerged from a side door of his mansion carrying an unconscious woman. She was tied from behind and tape was covering her mouth. I left my two men and tailed him in order to see what he was up to. He drove for about ten kilometers, got out, knocked her out, removed the handcuffs and the tape from her mouth and rolled her into a ditch. Then he drove back towards his chateau. I had pulled way over under some trees, and he drove by without spotting me. I rushed to the spot, and thank God I did, because he had pushed her into a ditch filled with water. I managed to get her out in the nick of time, but she was in a bad way. Christ, she was battered, bruised and getting hysterical. I radioed my guys to stay put and took her to a doctor I know outside Paris. He patched her up the best way he could and gave her a shot to quiet her. I eventually heard the whole story of her being beaten, raped over and over, and beaten some more. She had expected to be killed, but he chose the ditch routine."

Matt asked him who was taking care of her and, after some hesitation, Fred told him that he had taken her under his wing for the time being and that she was safely installed inside his country home, carefully watched over by his aging `aunt.

"She's quite the girl, Matt. She's a prostitute without a pimp for protection. I've talked her into quitting the sex trade, and told her that I would help her get a new start."

Matt was quiet for a few moments and, for to Fred's ears only, said that Herrick would soon get what he deserved. Matt told Fred that he would call him again the following week, and that payment for his services would be taken care of when he got back to Seattle. He thanked Fred for everything and disconnected the call.

He was disturbed by what had happened to the girl, but for now, he put it on a back burner and gave Nina the ok to cancel all of Frank Herrick's credit cards.

He took out his SAT phone to make three phone calls, to start the ball rolling.

At two thirty, Monday afternoon, just outside Paris, a phone rang three times in the now empty Chateau—then a screech—then the building exploded into a fiery ball, and by the time the fire and smoke had disappeared, the structure was obliterated. Half the citizens of Paris heard the explosion. Three fire halls responded.

The next phone calls triggered the explosives to Herrick's mansion and his drug lab. The resulting five thirty a.m. explosions, Monday morning, woke up a good part of LA, and all thought the city was under siege. Both structures were again obliterated. Matt was relieved that not a person had been killed or injured in the blasts.

Matt had Ryan drove to Los Angeles International Airport to locate and steal Herrick's gold Phantom Rolls, using one of the extra set of keys taken from his home only hours before.

All was accomplished, and now they patiently waited for Herrick and his five gunmen to arrive in about four hours.

Chapter 9

Jeff Harrigan was perhaps taking too much delight in what he was observing. Jazz and Bear were beside themselves. Frustration was building as to where the hell they were and how they would escape. At the very least, they were working together and obeying all the rules—with the exception of trying to escape. They were currently endeavoring to build a raft from fallen trees and driftwood and binding it all together with bits of rope and tree branches. Bear was trying to fashion a steering device by whittling a plank, using the only axe on the island. Results were pathetic, but at least it was giving them something to do.

"What are your thoughts about cutting the raft loose and sending it downriver?" Jeff had asked Matt during their daily phone schedule.

"I think it would be a great idea. Can you imagine their reaction?"

They both chuckled as to how Bear and Jazz would react.

"We'll be back in about a week with the next prisoners and their food supplies. I suggest we make two trips to the island. First the prisoners will be dropped off and then their supplies. I'll see you in about a week."

Matt signed off and Jeff continued to monitor the island. He waited for the two men to bed down for the night.

—

Meanwhile, back in Seattle, Matt's investigators were learning some interesting facts about Chester Bennett. His chosen profession was accounting, and for the past ten years, he had been working the books for a local Seattle mob, which were involved in prostitution, illegal gambling activities, drugs, extortion and smuggling. His major purpose was laundering millions of dollars each year and funneling the money into legitimate corporations around the country. He was good at this, and was well rewarded for his efforts. He deposited his earnings into his Cayman account. The mob money was also deposited into a Cayman account. Three days a week he was a legitimate accountant for Williams & James Financial, and for three days a week would work for the mob at McFerston & Freemantle, under their watchful eye. At the end of each working day, a gang member would put his meticulous ledgers and his laptop into a safe. The same procedure, in reverse, would be repeated when he started his next day of work.

However, all this laundering required much juggling and pressure, and often he became frustrated, angry and would frequently take his frustrations out on his wife—and others as well. Quite often he would be walking down a street, waiting for the right opportunity, and punch whoever was unfortunate enough to be in his vicinity.

He was just over five ten was not particularly handsome and anyone who met him quickly forgot his face. Chester kept himself fit at a local gym and jogged as well. Often, while on one of his runs in the park, he would gut punch an unsuspecting fellow jogger. He particularly loved doing this to female runners and usually caught them so unawares that they were unable to identify him. It was surprising how many of his victims were hospitalized by the viciousness of these attacks.

The investigators were able to assemble all this information into accurate reports and keep Matt informed by daily emails. They had been instructed to tap his phones and bug his offices and home. His home was now closely monitored, in order to keep watch on Chester Bennett's treatment of his family. The investigators were advised not to interfere with his various cruelties unless things got out of hand.

Currently, his wife Sara was holding an ice pack to a black eye she had received the previous evening. She was tired of these constant beatings. The worst part of it was that she was always caught unawares, as he always hit her when she least expected it. He seemed to take such pleasure in surprising her. Once he had snuck up behind her as she was bending over picking up some towels in the bathroom and he administered a vicious kick to her backside. This knocked her to the floor, and she hit her head against the bathtub.

"Hurts, doesn't it?" he said.

He loved to sucker punch her, usually in the kidney area or the stomach. Whenever Chester was home, she was so filled with terror, that she was developing an ulcer. Migraines were happening with increasing frequency.

She was aware of his mob connections, and knew he could always find her if she ever left him. He was careful not to touch their six-year-old Jeremy, and constantly reminded her that, should she ever threaten to leave, she and Jeremy would be hunted down and they would be badly beaten. She only had her brother, Barney, to turn to. The investigators longed to step in and beat Chester Bennett to a pulp, but orders were orders. They somehow knew that Matt had something in mind for this guy.

—

One arm of the Seattle mob that Chester Bennett worked for extended into New York and was headed by Jack Mostar. He ran their gambling operations and had the gift for making things happen. He generated a fortune for the mob and was well paid for his efforts. They had wisely decided to pay him a percentage of the take, which ensured that he would keep properly motivated. His expenses were his own to pay out of these earnings. His company name was Mostar Enterprises.

Mostar resided in a fabulous penthouse, just off Central Park. He ate at the best hotels, frequented the theaters of downtown Manhattan and lived like a king. His hobby was collecting cars and rare wine. It was not uncommon for him to pay over a hundred thousand dollars for a single bottle. He was a charming, well spoken and was frequently observed with beautiful women who couldn't get enough of him. They didn't suspect for a moment that he was one of the most ruthless men in New York.

He did not tolerate gambling debts beyond one month. His men would hunt down miscreant gamblers and mercilessly beat them, using metal pipes and baseball bats. These unfortunates had their kneecaps shattered or arms and legs broken. The message soon went out, to only gamble with money in hand. One man who was into him for half a million dollars was dealt with extremely harsh measures when he couldn't pay in his allotted time frame. He was beaten, kicked and had one of his arms broken. His wife was beaten and raped and his elderly parents were hounded continuously to have their son pay off his debt. The pressure caused the father to die of a heart attack and his mother to have a complete breakdown and had to be admitted to hospital for proper care. When the man still wouldn't (or couldn't) come up with the funds, he was taken to the top floor of a hotel and pushed to his death. A hotel security camera had caught them dragging him into one of the upper hotel suites just prior to the incident.

The hotel had contracted Secure Satellite Watchers to do surveillance of their upper class hotel guests. The cameras had caught it all. From the time they entered the hotel, entered one of the elevators and carried, what appeared to be a drunken buddy, into one of the suites. Shortly after, he fell to his death. The cameras had been well concealed and Mostar's men failed to notice them. When the police arrived, they reviewed the high quality camera images and identified the men in question as being under the employ of Jack Mostar. Jack Mostar and his men were charged and the trial was set six months following the murder. The case appeared to be ironclad.

Matt Chambers had also seen the images via a satellite feed and decided to follow the case to its conclusion. For a change, the justice system was going to nail this bastard.

Chapter 10

THE NEW YORK TIMES — Jack Mostar and his men exonerated for their alleged participation in the murder of a New York man who was supposedly pushed by them from a hotel balcony. Judge Allan T Petrick ruled the evidence as inconclusive due to the case lacking proof of anyone actually throwing him from the balcony and that the man could have simply committed suicide.

While Matt was waiting for Frank Herrick's arrival—due to arrive Tuesday morning at 2:00 a.m.—he used the time to scan his emails and catch up on what was happening in the newspaper world. The *New York Times* headline caught his eye and triggered his memory of what had taken place six months previous. To say that Matt was disappointed with the ruling was an understatement. He punched a Seattle number and spoke briefly with his current investigation team. Then he made a series of calls to New York. He also had Nina Sparrow perform some of her computer magic.

—

Herrick and his men were enjoying themselves in the first class section, although no other passengers seemed to be appreciating their behavior, and for good reason. They were drinking too much, were getting loud and generally making *Asses* of themselves. The stewardesses were becoming irritated with their familiarity and twice they had been touched in inappropriate ways. First class passengers seldom acted in this manner—*and with such rudeness too.* Thankfully, the passenger liner was starting its' descent into Los Angeles International, and they would be rid of the lot of them. *Such complete morons!*

The plane landed and slowly taxied to their terminal. Herrick and his men exited the plane, more than a bit inebriated and made their way to first class baggage pickup. Once there, they managed to snag one of the electric carts and left the terminal. One of Frank's men left the group standing beside their excessive baggage, in order to fetch the gold Rolls Royce, but soon returned without the car and made the announcement that it wasn't where it was supposed to be.

This vexed Herrick to no end.

"You two," he said snapping his fingers at two of his other men," go with him and find the fuck'n car so we can get out of here."

It was two a.m. Tuesday morning, and by this time they were all impatient, nauseated from consuming too much alcohol and exhausted, due to lack of sleep.

They returned empty-handed. The car had either been towed, moved or stolen. By now Frank Herrick was in a rage and told them to hire a limo to drive them to the estate. Frank was short on cash, so he went to a nearby bank machine to withdraw some currency and found that the machine rejected his card and then swallowed it. He was livid and asked one of his men to use one of their personal cards and withdraw cash for their ride. By two thirty, they managed to squeeze together into the rented Limo, along with luggage crammed into the trunk, between their knees and on their laps. Frank sat in the front passenger seat, distancing himself from the idiots behind him. *Imagine losing a fuck'n gold Rolls Royce Phantom!*

—

José Heraldo was scared! He had been driving for a living for five years now and had never experienced fear like he was experiencing right now. This Frank asshole sitting beside him in the passenger seat was one scary bastard. José had never been with anyone like this in his life, plus the guy was getting madder by the minute, and his bad temper seemed to emanate from him in waves affecting everyone in the Limo. There was little doubt that he was the boss.

Through his rearview mirror, he observed the other five, crammed into the back. The one described as Mitch, appeared to be the leader of the other four and was some cold looking dude. And his eyes! *Madre de Dios!* He had never seen such scary eyes. They seemed to look right into the soul. He was huge, at least six foot four, powerful and threatening. Then there was the one called Max whose face looked like someone had attacked him with a broken bottle; he had skewed eyes, making it impossible to look directly at him. He glanced at the one called Chris who had the look of a mean ferret. He was the shortest of the bunch and looked like he could move the quickest. Carl resembled a beanpole, handsome and intelligent-looking, almost like a schoolteacher, except for the fact that he had the foulest mouth that José had ever heard. Finally there was Brent, a bit taller than Chris, and by far the sharpest dresser of the group. He was in great shape, but looked like a sadistic killer and had a bad limp, probably from being shot or stabbed.

Ay Dios! If I make it out of this limo alive I am going back to school.

—

An hour and a half later, they arrived outside the now wrecked and wide-open Mansion gate. Yellow security tape crisscrossed the entrance. They were jolted out of their fugue by this totally unsuspected turn of events and were growing more uneasy by the second. Their weapons were all stored in the trunk of the Rolls—*wherever that fuck'n car had gotten to.* They told the driver to drive right through the tape and to proceed up the long driveway, slowly, with the lights off. José was getting real nervous.

They couldn't believe their eyes! The mansion had disappeared, and the only thing they could see was rubble, smoke and puddles of water everywhere. They were stunned. They exited the car and were now fully alert. Frank ordered the now panicky driver to: "stay the fuck inside the Limo" and yelled at Chris to: "fetch my fuck'n briefcase." The briefcase in question contained his cell phone, laptop, a file filled with vital information, and a notebook containing various codes. He set his briefcase onto his now upside-down empty safe, which had blown straight up into the sky and come back down, half burying itself into the ground. He took out his cell phone and called his security people.

At the same time José thought, *fuck this*. He reversed and squealed the car backwards until he lost sight of them, then quickly turned around to get the hell back to the city. He left them there without luggage and completely stranded at three-thirty in the morning. He would sell all the expensive luggage and contents to his Mexican cousin, who was in the fencing game. *José was leaving LA as soon as he could!*

Herrick's men wished they had gone with him. The clothes they were wearing were all they had left. All of their worldly possessions had been inside the mansion and in suitcases within the now departing limo. They were tired, hung over, hungry, feeling very vulnerable and worst of all, completely without any form of weaponry!

Frank Herrick's anger was volatile. The limo driver had left while he was still on his cell. The man on the other end of the call was frightened and was trying his best to tell Mr. Herrick the news—or lack of news—because everyone had been caught with their pants down. Their two security guards had disappeared, the mansion was toast, and the drug lab, which had been housed inside the dry cleaner building, was nothing but rubble after *that* explosion. He was also informed that his Paris Chateau was now rubble, after IT was blown sky high!

Frank was yelling by now, and asked the asshole at the other end why he hadn't been informed about the chaos that now greeted him. He was told that they had tried to reach him on his flight from Paris, but his cell was turned off. He was informed that everything that had taken place had happened when they were in mid-flight. Frank told the jerk on the other end of the phone to: "get them some fuck'n transportation, NOW!" The shaken man taking Frank's call replied that this would be taken care of immediately.

And just as he was starting to dial his lab manager's home number, Frank Herrick's cell phone quit working.

—

Matt was hidden in some shrubbery, some two hundred yards away, smiling grimly, at what he was witnessing. Herrick and his men were coming unglued and were definitely not in control. He had just given Nina the instructions over his cell to cut Frank Herrick's cell.

Ryan silently re-joined Matt in the shrubbery. After having driven Herrick's gold Rolls Phantom to a local police station containing a trunk full of illegal weapons and the bags of cocaine from the mansion. Nina had picked Ryan up, and, together, they had driven back to the hotel because she still had computer work to complete. Ryan drove to the airport and waited for the gang to arrive. He was amused at what had unfolded there.

Frank Herrick and his men had to wait nearly two and a half hours before two vehicles were delivered and they finally managed to regain some control over the plight they were in. Their first stop was to be King's Quick Delivery located in The Movat Tower. Matt and Ryan discreetly followed them.

—

They arrived at the office building at eight a.m. and warily emerged from the cars, looking like men who had slept in their clothes for days—unshaven and smelling of sweat and soot. They were a mess and all were in a foul mood. They entered the office building and rode up the elevator to the penthouse office. They needed money, weapons and control of their lives again. They also needed to find and kill those responsible for their plight.

Entering the office, they found the now-empty safe with its wide open door. Frank screamed in frustration! His cash was gone, as was his company ledgers, his two company laptops and all the guns! He was starting to lose control, and his men were growing uneasier by the second, wondering what else could go wrong.

They were soon to find out.

Frank had a sinking feeling as he withdrew his personal computer from his briefcase. The first thing he checked was his bank account, because cash infusion was now paramount. But to his horror, only one dollar remained in his LA bank account. He then frantically looked up his Cayman bank account.

His men, who were by now sitting in the office's various chairs and sofa, were witnessing all this and feeling the buildup of pressure in the room. The five men looked on as Frank called up his final bank account somewhere in the Cayman Islands. Frank sagged in his chair. It was all gone. A dollar was the only money remaining in the account.

Silence and foreboding filled the room!

They managed to feed themselves from the meager contents of the small office refrigerator and poured themselves stiff shots of whiskey. The badly shaken group was very quiet. It was finally decided they should at least get some sleep, mostly on the floors of the outer office. Frank barricaded himself in his office, with strict orders for them to be very vigilant. Frank, by now, was virtually punch-drunk and finally fell into a fitful sleep.

The five men in the outer office came to the realization that it was time to move on. The leader, Mitch, looked at Max for a long moment, then Brent and Chris, and finally at Carl, who was the only one sitting on the floor. Not a word was spoken; they all stood, went to the elevator door, and, when it opened, quietly filed out and made their way to one of the parked cars outside the office tower. Mitch drove, while Chris sat in the passenger side and the rest piled into the rear of the car. As they drove off, they didn't notice the two silent watchers in the dark van.

—

Frank awoke hours later in his dark office. Day had turned into night. He was troubled, helpless and beaten. He slowly made his way to his office door. He had to face his men. There was a lamp turned low in one of the far corners, and he noted that his men had left him to face his now empty, hopeless existence. As he was turning to return to his office, he heard a noise in the opposite corner. Two men were sitting in the dark facing him. The sound he had heard was a gun barrel tapping a coffee table. The gun was now pointed at his head.

"Who the *fuck* are you?"

The last thing he heard was a hissing noise. And something hit him in the neck. He fell to the floor and everything went black.

Matt pocketed the dart gun, and he and Ryan carried Herrick out of the building and into their waiting van.

They picked up Nina and the luggage and—with the unconscious Frank Herrick—drove to their waiting Learjet at Los Angeles International. They loaded everything without incident, carried Herrick and placed him inside the secret compartment. The Learjet lifted off and headed to Seattle.

Before a welcoming sleep, Matt made some more calls.

Chapter 11

Josh Willis was discreetly jogging far behind Chester, who had decided on a mid-morning run, and who twice had sucker-punched female runners. He tripped the first runner, as he was passing her, and the poor girl fell painfully to her knees, skinning them badly. The second of the females, who was running towards him, received a vicious punch to the mid-section, and went down heavily, curled up in a tight ball of agony. Chester stopped and kicked her in the back of her neck, and shoulders, and continued on.

Josh stopped to aide her and called 911 to send an ambulance. While waiting for help, he also called his partner, and informed him why he had ceased following the accursed Chester. His partner who was parked nearby, in turn, called his boss at surveillance headquarters and reported in. He was told to stay put and wait for Josh to rejoin him. and then head in for a briefing.

An hour later, the investigating team were putting their heads together as to how best to proceed and all were in complete agreement that this asshole was rapidly coming unglued. In reviewing the latest surveillance tape at Chester's office, it was obvious that he was under increasing pressure to satisfy the mob's latest money laundering scheme, which was evidenced by his recent escalation of violence. They were all concerned for the safety of Sara and her son.

The investigating agency managed to get through to Matt, who was currently on his return flight from Los Angeles, and were advised to closely observe Chester's home activities that evening. If things got out of hand, they were to enter the home, using any method of subduing him as they saw fit. Matt assured them that the man would soon be dealt with and they would be free of this sorry specimen of a human being.

It turned out that Chester did not go directly home that particular night, but instead checked into a local hotel. He paid the hotel in cash, avoiding any paper trail, as he was a careful man, especially with his mob involvement. He went to the hotel lounge for a few drinks. Josh followed him inside and sat at a distant table, keeping a watchful eye on him. It was obvious that the drunker the man got, the more obnoxious he was becoming. He was currently negotiating with the bartender to make arrangements to procure a prostitute. Chester tipped him a hundred dollar bill and told him he was checked into room 814. He then staggered out to the elevator, now so drunk that he was having trouble even pushing the up button. The elevator door opened and he fumbled his way up to his room.

Ten minutes later a woman entered the hotel, went into the bar for a drink and to confer with the bartender. While she was waiting for her drink, Josh walked over to her table and asked if it was all right if he could join her. Ever the businesswoman, she complied and Josh proceeded to have an eye-opening conversation with the prostitute. By the time they were finished talking, she quietly got up and left the hotel.

Chester, by now, had passed out in his room. Josh continued his hotel surveillance, called in for further instructions and was told to sit tight. His boss called Matt, whose plane was just touching down in Seattle and reported the latest news regarding Chester Bennett. Matt contemplated for a few moments before suggesting that Josh also rent a room under an assumed name, but to do so by paying cash. It was agreed that the name he was to use, would be Peter Clemmons.

They arrived at Seattle-Tacoma international at eleven p.m., and while the plane was being refueled, supplies for their northern trip were also loaded. Matt asked Nina if she was up to handling one more assignment.

"Of course," she said. "No problem at all."

She would accompany Matt to the hotel in his Explorer then they would later drive to Chester Bennett's office for a little *night* work.

Matt suggested that Ryan take two weeks off in order to spend time with his family. He handed Ryan an envelope that included four first class tickets to Disney World and accommodations at the Hilton Hotel. A chauffeured limo for the entire stay would be at their disposal. A healthy bonus was included. Ryan was thrilled and couldn't wait to break the news to his family.

At the hotel, Nina waited outside in the Ford Explorer while Matt joined Josh in his hotel room on the sixth floor. Their plan was for Josh to call Chester's room and inform him the prostitute was on her way up. They let the phone ring several times before a confused, hung-over Chester finally answered and informed him of the impending visit of the prostitute.

"The bitch sure took her fucking time getting here! I'll leave the latch open. Tell her to come in and wait on the bed. I'm going to freshen up."

They used the stairs and ran up the two floors to Chester Bennett's room, and while Josh went looking for a four wheeled laundry hamper, Matt let himself into room 814, his face covered by a balaclava. He sat on the edge of the bed, dart gun in hand, and waited a few minutes before Bennett emerged from the bathroom, fully dressed, drying his face with a towel.

"I hope you're prepared for some fun."

When he removed the towel from his face, he did a double take when he saw the hooded man sitting on the bed facing him while pointing a gun at his head.

"What the fuck?" he said, just before getting hit in the neck with a dart. Seconds later he passed out on the floor. Matt called Nina on his cell phone and asked her to drive to the side entrance of the hotel and wait.

Matt opened the door, just as Josh arrived with the laundry hamper, and wheeled it into the room. They removed some soiled linen, and together, lifted Bennett into the hamper. They covered him with soiled linen, pushed the cart into the hallway, and wheeled it to a freight elevator, located at the far end of the hotel corridor. They hit the down button to the basement, found the exit door and wheeled the cart outside. Because of the time of day not a soul noticed them leave.

Nina was waiting for them, and they loaded their victim into the back of the Explorer. Matt handed out latex gloves for the three to wear—no telltale fingerprints could afford to be left anywhere during the next phase of their operation. Josh took Chester's car keys from his pocket and located Chester's Lexus in the hotel parking lot and drove it to a nearby vacant lot and locked it up.

Nina and Matt followed in their van and drove Josh back to his car and asked him to proceed to Chester Bennett's home and quickly remove all company bugging equipment. He requested Josh to please keep everything very confidential, due to Bennett's mob affiliations. Matt thanked him for all his efforts and drove off.

Josh proceeded to do the debugging and was happy to get himself home and take some much needed time off. He was also relieved to be rid Bennett—*the sick son of a bitch*—and knew he would get what he deserved!

—

Matt drove, while Nina paid close attention to the next part of the plan, and soon they arrived at the office of McFerston & Freemantle. It was unguarded, but had very secure locks mounted into a riveted steel door. The windows were thick and looked to be bulletproof. The street was located in a quiet section of Seattle and devoid of traffic at four in the morning. Using the keys from Chester Bennett's pocket, they quickly let themselves into the front office area, which contained a secretary desk, six locked filing cabinets and a coffee making area. They unlocked the inner door to Chester's office, entered and quickly shut it behind them. The office was functional and contained two desks and several metal chairs. Cheap carpeting covered the floors. The room had no windows. A heavy, freestanding safe was located in the far corner of the office. The safe gizmo was again used on the safe, and was opened. It contained a laptop, four red ledgers, and a small leather notepad. These items were loaded into a duffel bag and the safe relocked. Matt then removed the agency bugs, pocketed them, and quickly left the building, locking all the doors as they departed. They drove in silence back to the airport and the waiting jet.

Nina seated herself inside the jet and accessed the mob's laptop while Matt and the copilot carried the sleeping Chester to the rear of the plane. Once there, a hidden panel was slid back, revealing a tiny space containing only a simple narrow cot. Lying on it was a sleeping Frank Herrick, hand-cuffed to the cot's frame. They shifted Herrick onto his side and managed to lay Chester Bennett also on his side facing Herrick. Bennett was hand-cuffed to the cot. Both would remain unconscious for another eight hours. Matt then fitted them with the specially designed hiking boots, and the soundproof space was resealed. A stack of supplies was slid in front of the now innocent looking panel.

Matt contacted Barney Satch and instructed him to proceed directly to the airport, using his own car, and join him inside the Learjet.

Nina, by now, had accessed the computer, using the various codes from the leather notebook, and revealed the mob's Cayman bank balance, which amounted to six and a half billion dollars. All was transferred into a ghost account and Matt again laid out which charities it all would be credited to, and again left one dollar in the account. She then assessed the mob's Seattle bank account, which amounted to over a billion dollars, and repeated the charity donation procedure.

The laptop, notepad, ledgers and a descriptive letter were put into a FedEx box, and Matt had it sent off to FBI headquarters in Washington, to the West Coast Crimes Division. It was sent anonymously to the head of the department, Wes Harrison. It was then that they finally removed their latex gloves.

Shortly before seven, Barney joined them. It was obvious that Nina was thrilled at seeing him once again. Barney had a smirk on his face and was beaming. The copilot brought coffee and hot croissants, and while they ate, the next phase of the plan was hurriedly unveiled.

Matt explained that Chester Bennett was soon to disappear and that Sara and her son had to be immediately moved to a penthouse suite he owned, overlooking Lake Washington. They were to drive to the private underground parking area and use the penthouse elevator. Matt suggested that Nina and Barney also move into the penthouse. He sat back faintly smiling, as he thought of the outcome. Barney and Nina looked at each other, and, after a few moments, without saying a word, both nodded. Time was of the essence, and the four had to be inside the penthouse by at least ten thirty a.m., because the mob would soon discover the disappearance of Chester, the ledgers and the incriminating notepad. At that point, shit would then hit the fan. Matt handed Barney a duffel bag containing one million dollars to do with as they saw fit. He gave a similar amount to Nina for her week's work. The untraceable money had come from Frank Herrick's mansion safe, back in LA.

Matt informed Barney that he had already anticipated Barney's yes answer and that a temporary replacement driver for his family had already been taken care of. They parted company just as the Learjet's engines started up.

US–Canada Customs were easily cleared, with only a few cursory questions pertaining to the supplies supposedly destined for the distant British Columbia fishing camp. As they cleared customs in Vancouver, early that afternoon, the Learjet rapidly ascended into a clear Canadian sky.

Chapter 12

It was early Monday morning, and time was of the essence. Barney opened the passenger door of his car for Nina and quickly went around to the driver's side, started the car and off they went.

He phoned Sara from the car, using a throwaway cell phone that Matt had given him before parting company at the airport. After three rings, a sleepy Sara answered her phone, and Barney wasted little time in explaining the situation to her. Sara was jolted awake at what he had to say. He asked her to please trust him and follow his exact instructions.

She was to get dressed and pack a gym bag with essentials only, get Jeremy dressed, leave the house immediately and slowly walk south towards a small shopping centre, located a few blocks away. He would approach the two of them in his car from behind, honk twice and they were to walk over to the car, climb into the back seat and they would drive away, avoiding any undue attention. He would explain everything to her later, when Jeremy was out of earshot. Naturally, Sara was very uneasy with all this cloak and dagger stuff, but she agreed to follow his instructions.

It was ten-thirty before Barney spotted the pair walking along the street. He honked twice and they hastily walked to the car and jumped into the backseat of Barney's vehicle. Jeremy was one happy kid because he could skip school and be with his uncle Barney too! The conversation was kept light and relaxed because of Jeremy. A half hour later, they drove into Matt's apartment parkade, unloaded the car and entered the private elevator to the penthouse.

And what a grand place it was! The penthouse boasted a spectacular layout, containing a spacious kitchen, four bedrooms, three bathrooms, an office, a TV room and a living room overlooking Lake Washington. It was completely furnished, and the décor was splendid. While Jeremy was happily installed into the video room, watching a TV program, Barney, Nina and his sister sat in the living room. Barney explained what was going on. Sara listened incredulously at what she was hearing. Chester would no longer be around, but they were to remain in the penthouse, out of sight, for about two weeks and then would be moved to another safe location. Nina watched Sara's reaction to all this and was relieved when she observed that Sara appeared quite relieved to be rid of Chester. Nina could see her start to relax, and for now, she and Jeremy would let themselves be under her brother's care. Barney excused himself and went to check on Jeremy.

During his absence, Sara and Nina chatted. Sara was dying to know about the relationship between Nina and her brother and was surprised that they had spent barely a day together! Nina explained that she was here at Matt's request, in order to help Sara and Jeremy. Nina would be sleeping in her own bedroom. Sara decided to let it go for now, but she sensed there was a lot more happening between the two of them and she wisely steered clear of the subject, at least for the present.

Nina asked Sara how she was coping with everything, so far. And that was when Sara lost it. Her pent-up emotions poured out and she started to cry. After a few minutes she calmed down and proceeded to tell Nina about her miserable life with Chester. She talked about the punches and the kicks, the constant threats and most of all the terror of having him in the same house. At least his cruel forms of sex with her had subsided in the recent months. Right now, she was relieved to be rid of him but had trouble believing he was finally gone. She was still very frightened that the mob would find her and do harm to her and Jeremy.

Nina decided at that moment, to make a difference in Sara's life, and during a lull in their conversation, put a little plan together and voiced part of that plan to Sara. First and foremost, a complete change of identity was required and a new wardrobe for both her and Jeremy. She also made notes of Sara and Jeremy's other needs. Sara was naturally concerned how she was to pay for everything, but Nina said that Barney would later explain how it would all be taken care of.

Barney entered the room right on cue and sat with them. It was decided the first priority was groceries. He would take care of this at once, excused himself and left Sara in Nina's capable hands.

Nina took time to develop more of her plan, took their clothes measurements and placed a few calls. As soon as Barney returned, she would have to make a trip to her own apartment. Nina had much to do. She had to pack, pick up her car, shop for their new wardrobe and drop by to see her parents.

Barney returned two hours later, laden with groceries, and while Sara and Jeremy helped put them away, Nina phoned for a taxi to take her to her apartment. Barney accompanied her to the taxi, gave her a hug, and thanked her for all she was about to do for them. The taxi drove off. *Barney was missing her already!*

Once at her apartment, she packed, carried everything to her car and went clothes shopping for the next two hours. She drove a short distance to her parents' home in a nearby suburb and was lucky enough to find them both at home.

Nina's mother was an elegant, tall, shrewd, perceptive lady with a great love of life. She kept herself active by working as a local makeup artist for a local theatrical group.

Her dad and mom were well matched. Her dad had always been quiet, attentive, patient, pensive and was a well-organized person. He ran a very profitable printing business and also worked closely with the Seattle police, making identity change documents for their witness protection program.

Nina asked for their help in regards to her present situation. They listened intently while she explained about her association with Matt and Barney and about Chester's mob affiliation and finally the cruelty he had inflicted on Sara. Nina believed a complete makeover was in order and a new identity was needed for Sara and Jeremy. She was strongly convinced that her parents were tailor-made to help her accomplish this goal.

Without hesitation, they both agreed to help and said they would drive out early the following morning. She hugged her thanks to both and drove off.

By the time she arrived back at the penthouse, Sara, Barney, and Jeremy were preparing the evening meal. They were all in great spirits. Nina performed a great balancing act in carrying in all the various bags and parcels, and spread them out on the living room floor. Barney accompanied her down to the garage to help her with the rest of her harvest. He shyly held her hand on the way down. Nina quite enjoyed the experience.

When they returned, they dumped everything else onto the living room floor, and Barney popped a special bottle of Perrier-Jouët champagne to celebrate this special occasion.

For dinner, they enjoyed a simple pasta dish, garlic toast and a wonderful spinach salad, which Jeremy helped prepare. Nina's contribution was a special dressing for the salad, which her mother had taught her to prepare during her teenage years. For dessert, big bowls of Jeremy's all-time favorite of fine Italian Spumoni ice cream.

Sara couldn't remember having so much fun, and her son appeared to be enjoying himself immensely too! After dinner, the contents of the various bags and packages were opened and distributed. It was great fun—not unlike Christmas. Nina had even picked up a pair of chinos, a patterned expensive shirt, two t-shirts, three pairs of boxer shorts, and a bathrobe for Barney and had correctly guessed his sizes. Nina told them of her visit with her parents and why they would be dropping by the following morning. They turned in early, as it had been an exhausting day.

As Nina lay in her bed, she was experiencing strong feelings about Barney, and unbeknownst to her, Barney was having similar thoughts about her. He was thrilled that she had thought to pick up clothes for him, as he had not had the chance to pack.

Barney awoke to the smell of coffee, and donning his new bathrobe, went out to investigate the source. He found Nina curled up on a couch in the living room, warming her hands on a mug of hot coffee, while looking out over Lake Washington. She was deep in thought. He startled her when he asked if he could join her. She gave him a smile of welcome and said she liked his new bathrobe. He helped himself to coffee and joined her on the couch.

Barney found he was comfortable in her presence and loved talking to her. He would also love to drag her into his bedroom and make love to her—but first things first. They talked easily to one other about their lives and dreams and were looking deeply into each other's eyes, when Jeremy came bursting into the room saying how hungry he was. The three prepared breakfast together.

Sara was awakened by the sound of their happy voices and went out to join them. She couldn't remember the last time she was so relaxed and alive!

Following breakfast, they all showered and dressed. Nina's parents buzzed themselves up right on time and joined the happy group. Her mom brought her large theatrical makeup-kit along with a couple of bulging shopping bags. Her dad was carrying a heavy cardboard file box.

Introductions were made, coffee was served and happy conversation ensued. Nina's mom, Maxine, captured everyone's attention with her makeup stories of some of the well-known actresses she had done work for. Shortly after, the women went into Sara's bedroom to start her makeover. Barney and Jeremy stayed behind to help Nina's dad, Sidney, get organized.

The three men conversed some more and decided to prepare some lunch. Sidney amazed them in the kitchen as he put together gourmet sandwiches and assembled a mouth-watering fruit salad. Barney and Jeremy helped by chopping the fruit and setting the table.

Two hours later, the ladies reentered. The men couldn't believe the result! Sara did not resemble the old Sara at all. She had been turned into a very striking woman. Her drab shoulder length dark hair was now beautifully styled and cut short. Furthermore, she was now a spectacular blonde. The professional makeup brought out strikingly blue eyes, her few wrinkles had disappeared and her lips now supported bright red lipstick. Jeremy hardly recognized her. The wardrobe that Nina had picked for her was perfect. She was dressed in a red suit with black buttons, a simple string of pearls, black nylons and red high heel shoes. The transformation was stunning. Sara felt like a queen!

After the oohs and aahs, Sidney took over and performed his magic. He photographed Sara from the shoulders up, took down all her information, determined her needs, and promised her that she would receive a new identity within the week. He repeated the same procedure with Jeremy. The only thing still required, was a change of name. Lunch was served amid laughter and bubbly conversation.

Nina fired up her laptop and found a website of North American first names for Sara and Jeremy, to help them choose new identities. Sara settled on Amanda, while Jeremy chose Tyler. Sara and Jeremy chose their new family name together and settled on *Winters*. Amanda Winters and Tyler Winters sounded good to them, and they were happy with their choice. Jeremy certainly was, as had never liked his father or the way he had treated them. *He was as happy as his Mother!*

Sidney and Maxine said their goodbyes and promised to stay in touch. Maxine was asked to drop by for another makeup session as soon as Sidney had their new identities completed.

It had been a very productive day, and all collaborated in the making of dinner. When it was time for bed, all retreated to their rooms in a much happier frame of mind.

Two hours later, Nina quietly knocked on Barney's door. He was still awake, and happily invited her to join him. She observed that he slept in the nude, so, in the spirit of cooperation, she disrobed and snuggled in beside him.

Chapter 13

Brilliant sunshine bathed the courtyard of mob boss Gino Danelli's country villa, located on Seattle's Sunset Hill, overlooking Puget Sound. It was a crisp November morning. Gino, dressed in a silk Missoni bathrobe, espresso in hand, was enjoying the start of a new day on his patio overlooking the tranquil bay.

His wife and two children were currently holidaying in Italy with her parents, and he sorely missed them. They were only halfway through a month long vacation.

His thoughts turned to his recently acquired eastern property division on the east coast, which was producing fantastic profits. The man running it, Jack Mostar, was an excellent administrator. Gambling was a pure profit venture and in Jack's hands, it was doing well and growing exponentially, since he had been given a percentage of the action. The only cloud in the horizon was the murder charges being laid against Jack and his men. That had been a bad blunder, but Gino had already pulled a few strings to get the charges dropped. At the proper time, he would have a chat with the man.

All of the other divisions were also yielding great profits. The drug division continued to beat prior year results, the three casinos' growth always surprised him, and prostitution was always in demand. And finally, there was the extortion and smuggling division ran by his lieutenant, Bruno Cesare. Bruno also served as head of security and was expected to arrive shortly for their nine-thirty morning meeting.

Bruno, however, was running late, which was highly unusual for him, and another hour passed before his arrival. A very serious and bewildered

Bruno stood in front of Gino, looking more than a little uneasy. Danelli patiently waited for Bruno to divulge his report.

Bruno finally got it out, as he had just returned from the McFerston & Freemantle office, responding to a call from their frantic office-manager who had informed him that Chester Bennett had failed to show up this morning.

"I tried raising him on his cell and home phone," Bruno said, "but no one answered. I sent a car over to his place to investigate, but they found no one home. And when they broke in, they found that someone had hurriedly packed some bags and moved out. Chester's stuff didn't appear to be touched, so we assumed his wife and kid have skipped out. I started to smell a rat, so I had the office safe opened. It was empty, and I came directly here."

Silence greeted this news. Gino finally suggested they go down to his den computer and check things out. They proceeded to his elaborate office. The library walls were lined from floor to ceiling, filled with a vast array of beautifully bound books, many of which were rare and irreplaceable. Elaborate glass doors enclosed all books. A Plush Persian rug with design patterns of gold and ivory graced the floor. The desk was made of intricate rare hardwoods and dominated the center of the room. Gino pressed a hidden button, and a computer emerged from the center of the desk, codes were entered, and bank information was displayed. The Seattle account showed a balance of one dollar—roughly a billion dollars, gone! He brought up the Cayman account, and the balance also showing a total of one dollar. Gino stared at the screen. Six and a half billion dollars had disappeared!

Bruno, seated in front of the desk, was not yet privy to what Gino was looking at and was confronted by silence. Gino was in deep thought. He slowly opened the top left hand drawer of his desk and withdrew a pad of paper and a gold pen and proceeded to make some notes. After ten minutes of writing, he looked up and stared at Bruno.

"You are not to write down any of what I am about to say," he said. "Commit it to memory."

"I understand, Mr. Danelli."

"Both the Seattle bank account and Cayman account have been cleaned out."

Bruno flinched and starting to sweat with fear of what was to come next.

"*No one* is to know about this! Naturally, this cannot be reported to the police, so here is what I want done.

"First, Chester Bennett is to be found and brought here. I want to know whom this cocksucker has been in contact with. He hasn't the smarts nor the guts to pull this off on his own. I want you to call in some favors and have fingerprints taken at McFerston & Freemantle, his home and his car. And I want his wife and kid found and brought here. I want all our resources to comb the airports, train stations, and car rental agencies. I want his credit cards tracked and his phone records pulled on all his calls during the past year. I will pay a reward one million dollars to whoever brings him to us, but only on the condition he is delivered to us alive.

"I also want our guard at McFerston & Freemantle grilled, and I want answers. He must have heard or seen something! I want answers within forty-eight hours. Tell all our people to stop whatever they're doing and get me *some fucking answers!*"

Bruno understood. He quietly got up and departed.

Within two hours, twenty-three cars containing three men per car, began combing all parts of Seattle, each with a specific assignment. Bennett's home and McFerston & Freemantle were thoroughly searched, but only after two officials who owed Bruno a few favors, took fingerprints. Then Gavino Basta, who was in charge of security at McFerston & Freemantle, was grilled. Bruno's team only had to break four of Gavino's fingers and administer some intensive beating before it was determined he was innocent of any wrongdoing.

Ten teams covered all exits from the city, looking for a black Lexus bearing Chester's license plate number, and again, favors were called in to determine if, and how, Bennett had left the city.

A team of computer specialists combed through all ingoing and outgoing calls placed by Chester during the past year. They also pulled his Visa and American Express accounts and searched all charges. They went back two years. They checked his Seattle bank account and his Cayman account, checking each and every debit and credit.

Three teams were assigned to find Sara Bennett and her son. Neighbors, friends, acquaintances, service people, hairdressers, businesses and gas stations were intensely questioned and ordered to keep their mouths shut!

The remaining teams combed the entire city and the only thing they came up with was Bennett's Lexus parked in an empty parking lot. Fingerprints were lifted from various parts of the car. The only fingerprints they found belonged to Chester, and the entire car contained only his gym bag filled with jogging cloths and runners, and a gun in the glove compartment registered to Chester Bennett.

Thirty hours later, they received the fingerprint results from McFerston & Freemantle. All prints were traced to Gavino Basta, Chester Bennett, their secretarial staff and the cleaning staff. Bennett's home yielded only three sets of prints, that of Chester, Sara and the boy.

Forty-eight hours later, Bruno was again sitting in front of Gino Danelli giving him his verbal report. After all their efforts, they came up with absolutely nothing! Chester Bennett, his wife and son, had simply vanished!

Gino Danelli slowly opening a drawer containing his gun. He inner rage was peaking, and he was going to kill Bruno for his failure.

At that moment the front door chimed. He re-closed the drawer containing the gun and went to answer the door himself. He had dismissed his servants for the day in anticipation of his meeting with Bruno.

When he opened the door, four armed FBI agents confronted him, and had a warrant for his arrest. They also had a warrant to search his villa. He was handcuffed and led to one of the waiting cars. Bruno was also brought in for questioning.

Boxes of files, ledgers, his computers, weapons, the contents of his desk, and sixteen bags of cocaine were found and loaded into the FBI van.

Chapter 14

At five in the afternoon, the Learjet landed at the northern British Columbia hunting lodge. It touched down smooth as silk and taxied to a small hanger. The motors were cut, and silence descended on a delightful winter wonderland between two mountain ranges. The beginning of November this year was off to a cold start, and the current temperature was minus ten degrees Fahrenheit. The runway was well cleared and maintained by a man that had come with the lodge when Matt had purchased it a few years previous. Glen Nielson served as the lodge custodian when it was void of visitors. The man was loyal, knew how to maintain the equipment, required to keep the runway clean and well maintained. A truck with an attached snowplow served to keep the runway clear of snow. He was in his mid sixties, a solitary man and for whatever reason, loved the isolation. He lived in a small cabin near the lodge.

Matt arose and went to check on his two hostages. He slid the panel back, revealing the two sleeping men, who were beginning to stir. He removed a syringe from his briefcase and administered a reduced dose into both men's arms, which would induce another twelve hours of sleep. As had been done to the previous and future captives, he administered a saline drip to keep both men properly hydrated.

Jeff Harrigan rode out to meet them on a snowmobile, pulling a large attached trailer. He strode over to Matt and greeted him with a huge smile of welcome and the two men shook hands. The pilot and copilot helped them unload the supplies and the sleeping prisoners. They made their way to the hunting lodge, parked inside the lodge garage and closed the overhead door. The garage was heated, and they left the two unconscious men handcuffed to the trailer and made their way inside to partake in a huge breakfast prepared by Jeff. He had outdone himself by providing them with a mound of pancakes, scrambled eggs, bacon and a stack of toast. Their coffee mugs were filled from a huge pot, containing delicious coffee. All were happy to have finally arrived and looking forward to spending four days of relaxation—and a bit of work, of course. They still had to successfully install two more captives onto the island.

Bob Cummings had been Matt's pilot since the beginning and was fiercely loyal and dedicated. He was in his mid forties, tall, ruggedly handsome and serious. He sported a neat, close cut, salt and pepper beard. He had fierce blue eyes, a square chin and wore his well-tailored uniform with distinction. Matt had met him during his army days on a flight out of Colorado. They had hit it off well, and when Bob's stint was over, he came to work for Matt as his full time pilot.

Dan O'Malley was the copilot and had been hired by Bob straight out of the Army, two years previous. He was opposite to Cummings in stature, hearty and robust, almost handsome, five foot six and built like a tank. He and Bob loved flying together. Dan had started out as an army mechanic and had specialized in repairing jet airplanes. He could fix anything. Bob Cummings had taught him how to fly and he had become a well-qualified co pilot.

All the men present, believed in what Matt was trying to achieve. Pull scum from society and isolate them without the benefit of highly paid lawyers and judges who were told to ease up putting crooks into the already overloaded penal system, or by letting them serve only short sentences. The captives on the island more than deserved their isolation.

As they sat drinking their coffee, it was decided that Matt and Jeff would wait until midnight to pilot their boat, supplies and prisoners to the island. The river was deep and fast flowing and wouldn't freeze over, which was the reason Matt had chosen this remote setting.

For now, all retired to their rooms to catch up on some much needed sleep. Prior to drifting off, Matt's thoughts turned to his family.

Kirsten was doing a fine job of raising the children. Sam was now twelve, and Mia was nine. She frequently took them to the marina where she worked and they would watch while she swam with the dolphins and care for all manner of sea-life and taught them how to feed them. The kids were starting to have a real affinity for all sea creatures. By the time Matt would arrive home for dinner, Sam and Mia would enthusiastically tell him about their day with their mother. They were doing well in school too and seemed to have inherited their parents' enthusiasm for higher learning. Sam was just starting seventh grade, while Mia was starting fourth grade. Matt noticed a difference in Sam since the loss of his school chum, but he was slowly getting over it, and the experience would probably serve to strengthen him later on.

Since moving to Seattle, Kirsten became very active in the preservation of marine life. She was heavily involved in fighting to keep the huge fishing conglomerates as far away from these western shores as possible. It was like trying to stop the tide. The world has always been so greedy in decimating the fish populations of the oceans.

She was appalled at how government worked—or in most cases *didn't* work. Too many people who failed to make it in the business world had became politicians and rapidly learned how to squander the citizens hard-earned tax dollars. Budgets were never met due to various corruptions. It was a tired axiom; five percent tried to make a positive difference and ninety-five percent thwarted those efforts.

The justice system was failing and served only to make lawyers and politicians richer and society weaker. Prisons were overcrowded by as much as two hundred percent. The rich were seldom convicted, and when they were, the sentence was usually a reduced one, or a paltry slap on the wrist, by doing some form of community work. The prison system was built for comfort, and few inmates were made stronger by being confined within the system.

They both agreed that the failing political climate was antiquated and respected by few. Judges were becoming corrupt, while being bought and paid for by the rich and powerful. The judicial system was long overdue for an overhaul.

Kirsten was aware that Matt was trying to make a difference, and she respected that.

Matt set his mental clock to wake at eight p.m. and sank into a deep dreamless sleep.

He woke up refreshed, took a quick shower and brushed his teeth, but didn't bother to shave. He knocked on the door to the security room, entered and found Jeff monitoring the two island prisoners. It was too dark outside, but the cameras were beaming clear images of the men inside the cabin and every word was being received as clear as a bell.

"How did our little friends react to the losing of their raft?"

Jeff chuckled. "Pretty much as I expected. They became angry and cussed a lot, but I suspect that they were probably relieved at not having to attempt the river. They settled down within an hour and went about their usual routine. Remarkably, they seem to be getting along with each other."

The four met later in the large kitchen, and Matt and Bob made sandwiches and coffee. For dessert they demolished a delicious apple pie that Jeff had made the day before. They sat—at ease in each other's company— and discussed the evening plans.

Matt paired off with Bob and went for an evening walk, while Jeff and Dan washed the day's dishes and cleaned up the kitchen. The night was clear, and they decided to take a walk in the moonlight. All was silent, and the stars and moon were something to behold. The scrunch of the crisp snow beneath their feet was very soothing. As they walked, Bob looked over at Matt.

"Do you think you'll make a difference?" he asked

After a moment, Matt responded. "The men we've brought here are well organized at what they did, and whoever steps in to take over in their absence will make mistakes, get caught along the way and hopefully punished. I feel that I've taken some powerful evil people out of the equation and there will be a lot of uneasiness out there as a result. And lastly, it's great to have them finally pay for their sins and suffer, as they deserve. So far, I have no regrets."

They continued their walk, each in deep thought.

At eleven thirty, Matt and Jeff planned their roundabout trip to the island and arrived at the river's edge a half hour later and transferred the sleeping men into the waiting vessel. The alternate electric motor was started and would enable them to run silent. They pushed themselves free. It took another half hour to approach the lower uninhabited part of the island, the motor was switched off a few feet from shore, and the boat gently touched the island and the craft was secured.

Jeff turned on his SAT phone and brought up the GPS, so they could determine where the previous prisoners were located. The boot implants were doing the job and indicated that the two men were inside the cabin, probably fast asleep.

They unloaded the two prisoners and carried them towards a large spruce, about thirty feet from shore, and secured their wrists with rope and then tied the other end of the rope to the same spruce tree. They covered the two with blankets, to prevent them from freezing while they slept. A jackknife secured a note to the tree. They returned to the mainland to pickup the supplies and when they returned, carried them within a few feet of the sleeping pair. A small windup flashlight was placed on top of one of the stacks of supplies. Matt and Jeff carefully erased all evidence of their visit, re-boarded their vessel, and motored back to the hunting lodge.

Chapter 15

Frank Herrick was desperately trying to piece together where he was. He knew he was somewhere cold and quiet and very dark. He thought he heard wind blowing through trees and the faint sound of running water. He also knew he was hurting in several places. His neck, both arms and his left leg ached. He had a splitting headache. His eyes were throbbing. His mouth was dry and he was starving.

Frank was in a murderous mood as he tried to remember the son of a bitch that shot him—only he couldn't recollect a face. He only remembered a funny sound followed by a sharp pain in his neck and had a faint memory of falling and blacking out. Someone was going to pay, and pay dearly. Then, with gathering clarity, he remembered the horror of his now blown up mansion; the asshole Limo driver leaving them all stranded; being picked up and driven to his office only to discover the empty bank accounts; sleeping in his office and waking up to discover that his men had deserted him and finally the two men in the dark corner of the reception area.

Oh yes, payback is coming.

He found himself covered with a blanket and although it was cold, he was warm enough. Gloves and heavy boots were at least keeping his extremities warm but he did wonder where the gloves and boots had come from. He heard a moan from a man beside him, and Herrick went very still as he tried to make out who it was.

—

What the hell is going on?

Chester Bennett was emerging from a bad dream, only to discover a nightmare. *God, I am so sick I can hardly think.* His back was killing him, and he was cold and hungry. His mouth felt like dog shit rolled in gravel. For some reason he was wearing gloves and heavy boots. His stomach was so queasy.

He turned onto his side and spewed vomit onto the face of *Frank Herrick!* The sound of cursing filled the night, and a raging Herrick leapt up and began beating him with bound fists. Chester rolled over and went into a fetal position to avoid the deadly blows. Herrick started kicking the inert man in the side and trying, at the same time to wipe the vile vomit from his face. He was like an enraged animal. He soon had to stop though, as he too started to feel sick. He managed to control his heaving stomach and started taking deep breaths in order to get himself under control.

Why the fuck am I tied to a fucking tree?

Things were not going well for the LA crook. He reached down and pulled the cowering Chester Bennett to his feet and was getting ready to beat him all over again before realizing he'd better stop, lest he dropped from sheer exhaustion and hunger. *First things first!* He managed to get himself under some semblance of control and pushed the man who had puked on him up against a tree.

"Who the *fuck* are you, and where the hell are we?"

"I don't know," Chester said. "And I don't fucking care because I feel like dying, so leave me the *fuck* alone!"

Strangely this got through to the raging Herrick, and he managed to calm himself and take stock of their situation.

He noticed a pile of packages and boxes stacked a few feet from them, and managed to get close enough to inspect the two stacks. Perched within reach, he could make out the outlines of what appeared be a flashlight. He grabbed it and saw that it was a small windup flashlight. Frank cranked the handle a dozen times and flicked the switch and a small beam of light shone through the darkness. The first place he pointed it was at Chester Bennett's pasty white face. He was of average height, with a plain face, and appeared to be in reasonable shape, but for some reason Herrick didn't think much of him as a man. In fact, he came across as a coward of sorts. Next, he shone the light at the rope tethering his wrists to the spruce tree. It was then that he saw a pocketknife securing a piece of paper to the tree. He walked up to the note and, with the aid of the flashlight, started to read.

Hello Assholes!

How does it feel to be on the receiving end for a change? Read this carefully…

When he was finished, Frank Herrick read the note again—in disbelief. "Well what does it say?" Bennet asked, annoyed. "Read the goddamn note yourself!" Chester walked over, took the flashlight from Herrick, and read. "What the fuck?" he said when he was done. "Let's get to the fuck'n cabin before we freeze to death," Herrick said, and both men wrapped their blankets tightly around their bodies and started walking. Within minutes they reached the cabin and Frank threw open the door. The startled men inside were having their early morning coffee. They said nothing but simply stared at the newcomers who smelled of vomit and sweat. One was bruised, battered and pale, while the other looked like he would gladly kill either of them at any moment and was presently glaring murderously at them. Jazz had never known the kind of fear he was feeling in this man's presence. Jazz was afraid all over again, and his bowel clenched and he emitted a loud, foul fart. The three men all looked disgustedly at him.

"If you have to shit, get the fuck outside!" barked Herrick—which only made matters worse, eliciting a machinegun, burst of farts from the terrified man.

Frank Herrick walked over, grabbed him, and promptly propelled him outside, kicking him in his backside, in order to hurry him along. He slammed the door shut.

Jazz found himself suddenly in a quandary. He had no coat. He was freezing, plus he had to relieve himself. So priority took over, and he rushed to the river.

Inside, Frank looked at the other ugly asshole, and demanded a drink of water. Bear, who was a bit mystified with this unprecedented hostility, went to fetch a cup of water. Herrick drank thirstily, and when Chester asked for a drink too, he was told by Bear to get his own fuckin' glass of water! Frank then demanded to know where the next note of instruction was located and sat down to read it. When he finished, he looked at Bear and asked him how he got here? Bear, more or less repeated the same story that Frank had experienced about a pain in the neck prior to passing out and awoke the same way he had.

Just then there was a timid knock at the door, and Frank yelled that Jazz could enter only if he stopped with the fuck'n farting. Jazz timidly opened the door, entered, and proceeded to the stove to warm himself.

Chester finally spoke up and asked for something to eat. Bear told him where the food supplies were kept. When Chester emerged from the pantry, he looked a little mystified and was carrying a package of some kind of powdered substance. He asked what the hell it was, and Jazz, wanting to redeem himself, replied that he would prepare some food for them. All watched him as he went through the motions of putting together a meal of sorts. When he was finished, he served it up at the table and stepped back. While Herrick and Chester hungrily wolfed it down, Jazz poured them a coffee and retreated to his bunk.

All were wary of Frank Herrick and nervously awaited his next harangue. They didn't have long to wait. He asked them about the supplies stacked back beside the huge tree, and, having read the note, asked if this was the usual monthly allotment of food assigned. Bear nodded yes, and was told that he and Jazz were to go and haul it to the cabin. When they started to protest, Herrick said in a deadly voice that he and his so-called partner were too cold to venture out in the cold so soon. They reluctantly agreed to carry out the task, donned parkas and mitts, and without a word, left the cabin.

Herrick turned to Chester: "Do not utter a fuck'n word!" Then he took off his shirt and proceeded to wash the filth from his body. He hunted down a shirt from the supply room, put it on and felt a bit better. Then he started to look for something to shave with, but nothing of this nature presented itself. He did find a toothbrush and toothpaste and cleaned his teeth for the first time in days. He looked over at Chester and told him to clean himself up, because he stank of vomit. Chester complied, and a hate for Herrick started to build.

Jazz was in a mood and grumbled all the way to where the new supplies were stacked. Bear told him to shut the fuck up and get the supplies back to the cabin before they froze. They each made two trips and stored the provisions inside the storage room. They needed a hot cup of coffee to help warm them, but found that the water that had been warming on the stove, had been used for bathing by the two new assholes. When they grumbled about this, Herrick told them to put some more water on the stove. They were starting to get irritable and told Herrick that more water had to be hauled in from the river. Herrick, already in a foul mood, told them to get the fuck down to the river and get some more. Again, they put on parkas and mitts, picked up two empty buckets, and—again—obeyed.

Bear and Jazz were starting to get pissed with this prick. Bear voiced his opinion, and Jazz very quietly asked if they were going to take much more of this. Bear didn't comment, but he was thinking the same thing. They dipped the buckets into the freezing river and carted the full buckets back to the cabin.

Not a word was spoken by anyone when they returned. They removed their parkas and mitts for the second time and proceeded to fill the pan on the stove. Now they discovered that they were almost out of wood.

"It's your turn to help out with the chores, so how about going for some wood? Like the instructions said, we—"

"*Fuck* the instructions, I'm getting real tired of all you pricks, so I'm going to say this one more time. Go do what has to be done, and don't fuck'n bother asking again. And take this other piece of shit with you to help bring in your fuck'n wood."

For the third time, all donned their parkas and mitts and silently left to fetch the wood, but by now they were incensed at being ordered around and decided what they would do about it.

Frank Herrick was proving once more that he was alpha of the pack, and it was high time to start organizing these turds to start towing the line. He was starting to plan his next move when they returned bearing armfuls of wood and dumped it inside the woodbin. For all his intelligence, he failed to realize how hard he was pushing them. The pressure of the last few days had affected him badly and he wasn't thinking logically. He was starting lose control of his emotions and the pressure of what he had gone through in recent days was badly affecting him.

The men removed their parkas and mitts and silently approached Herrick. It was Bear who finally broke the silence.

"We've known you now for just over two hours and we have already had enough of your shit; from now on, you're going to help with the chores and start doing your fair share."

Frank stood and glared into the eyes of the three men in turn. He rage was affecting his judgment. *Time to put these fuck ups in their place.*

He started to yell once more.

"First of all—"

And that's when Jazz hit him with the axe handle.

Herrick managed to move his head just in time, and the blow that *might* have killed him almost dislocated his shoulder. The other three men began venting their own pent up frustrations and started to rain blows to his head, shoulders and body. Herrick fell to the floor and was kicked into unconsciousness.

Later, when he came to, he found that he was tied to his bunk. He kept his eyes closed for fear of receiving further blows. He was in agony and started to wonder what he had done to arrive at this pitiful state. *First I lose everything in LA, now this.* He had a sudden realization of how those prostitutes felt during their beatings. Frank Herrick had finally hit rock bottom.

Chapter 16

Wes Harrison, supervisor of FBI's West Coast Racket's Division, was in a quandary.

What the hell is going on? First, Frank Herrick's mansion in LA is blown to smithereens and the same thing happens to his Paris Chateau. Furthermore, the lab explosion looks like it's connected to Herrick as well. Then Herrick disappears, his five henchmen disappear, and now there is evidence that his bank accounts have been drained.

Then Seattle's mob kingpin Gino Danelli's ledgers, laptop and notepad are anonymously sent to FBI headquarters with an accompanying letter explaining whom it belonged to. Danelli's bank accounts had also been drained. His lieutenant, Bruno Cesare, won't say a fucking thing and now the goddamn accountant, Chester Bennett, has disappeared, along with his wife and son. Jesus, I don't need all this!

At least the evidence from Danelli's residence was positive, particularly his desk notepad, showing the instructions that had been noted regarding the Bennett search. Gino's computer also yielded excellent information about the men who answered to him and the amounts paid to them—big surprise, the mob members make ten times what I make!

Of course, no one is talking, least of all, Danelli.

At least we have enough on Gino Danelli, Bruno Cesare, and numerous gang members to put them all away for a long time.

With Danelli's bank accounts showing zero balance, there was no way on earth that bail would be granted to any of them!

Whatever was going on had been well planned, and as a bonus, his department would receive the credit for nailing Danelli and his mob— *always nice when these things fall in your lap*—but who, or what, was behind all this? So far, not even a hint was evident as to who forwarded the vital information.

The FBI investigators knew that military explosives caused all the explosions in LA and Paris.

The good news was that the drug trade on the West Coast was in shambles—and would remain so if he had anything to do with it. A lot of coincidental happenings were taking place, mostly positive in nature, but Wes Harrison was still on the hook to find who was behind all of this.

The big drive came from FBI higher-ups, who wanted drugs kept to a minimum now that they finally had momentum on their side. The Senate had granted them more funds to keep drugs out. It seemed to Wes that everything was too pat, too well planned?

A senior aide was buzzed in to give him a report as to some of the whys and who's of the latest happenings. He also brought three newspaper articles to review. The aide was invited to have a seat and spend a few minutes.

"Coffee?" Wes asked.

"Yes. All right," the man said. "Cream two sugars."

Wes took his coffee black. He served the coffee and took a seat beside the aide, on one of the comfortable office chairs.

"So, you've been looking at everything. Does it not seem a little strange to you? I mean, what do you make of it all?"

The aide shrugged and took a sip of his coffee before answering.

"My take on it is this: why look a gift horse in the mouth? Why waste time tracking down a person—or persons—responsible for so much good. What's to be gained? Why not simply take advantage of the situation and double down on our effort to keep drugs to an absolute minimum. The folks behind this are probably too clever to be caught in any case. And if we *were* to catch him—or them—what would we be comfortable charging them with? Personally I would want to shake their hands."

Wes understood that all right. He nodded and sipped his coffee.

"And what if we are dealing with some sort of vigilante?" Wes asked.

"So what if we are? The good far outweighs the bad, don't you think? My opinion, for what it's worth, is to simply leave it alone and continue focusing on more important issues."

These were good answers, so he thanked the aide for his opinions and assured him that he would take them under advisement. Wes got up and walked him to the door.

He returned to his side of the desk and thought about what the aide had said. Deep inside, he wanted to agree, but the FBI side of him was having trouble in arriving at a safe conclusion. He would, however, concentrate on the bad guys for now—but he would remain alert in regards to who this do-gooder really was.

After a few more minutes contemplating all that was on his plate, he perused the newspaper articles that his aide had left on his desk. His eyes widened a little at what he read, and he spent the next half hour reading the publications.

THE NEW YORK TIMES — Billions in Anonymous donations to various charities throughout North America and Canada. Sources mystified as to who is responsible for this unprecedented generosity.

THE WASHINGTON POST — Who is responsible for contributing unheard amounts to various charities throughout North America? A mystery in the making. Overwhelming generosity welcomed by many organizations.

THE DENVER POST — Local Charity groups benefit from anonymous donor. Millions contributed by generous benefactor enables many impending programs to move forward. Countless to benefit!

Shit, more coincidence?

Wes Harrison did not believe in coincidence. Something just wasn't right. The norm was not working here at all. He decided to visit Gino Danelli, where he was presently being held.

—

Gino Danelli was incensed and confused. *Where the hell did I go wrong?* He had been asking himself the same question over and over. He was not a stupid man, as was evidenced by his rapid rise to the top of the heap in a short period of time. In just ten years he had put together a strong organization—and it took mere days to lose it all. He would begin again, but this time with no stupid mistakes. *If I could only get my hands on that fucking accountant, I would waste little time in finding out what happened! As soon as I'm free, I'll deal with that cocksucker.* He shuddered to think what his wife was going to do when she finds all this out—and she was due home in two weeks!

His thoughts were interrupted when Wes Harrison again paid him a visit. *Fuck, this is all I need.* Gino was handcuffed from behind and sat facing the agent across a metal table. He looked coldly at Harrison and asked him when he was up for bail—*so I can get out of this shithole.*

Wes simply stared back at him while he tapped his fingers on the table surface.

"Is there anything else you want to tell me, Danelli? Now is your chance."

"I am not telling you a fucking thing, you prick. Now what about my bail hearing?"

Wes had seldom looked into colder eyes. He told Danelli the truth.

"Your bail has been denied! The attending judge has ruled that we have too much evidence to release you. You'll be going to trial, and I can assure you, that you will be behind bars for the rest of your miserable fucking life."

Danelli replied with cold calmness. "Mark my words, when I get out, I am going to make *everyone* pay dearly for what I am going through. I'm NOT fucking guilty!"

Wes quietly got up out of his chair, looked at Gino with equally cold eyes.

"Not in my lifetime, asshole!" he said and calmly walked out of the room.

For the first time in his life, Gino Danelli realized the true meaning of fear.

Chapter 17

They were airborne once again, this time on their way to New York. Matt favored New York for its dedication to the Arts, and its many theaters with their myriad of stage shows. Through the years, he had done a lot of business here. A Space Security Watchers office branch was located there, and the growth there was the strongest of all his enterprises. He had just completed a call to Charles Freemont, vice president of the Eastern division, and Matt would be meeting with him on his arrival.

Charles's work was exemplary, and he had been a former employee of his father's. Charles had helped pioneer Secure Security Sentries. Then he became interested in satellite technology and strongly believed they could revolutionize security around the world. Countries were demanding stronger security, and Matt's company was in a prime position to fulfill these requirements. In short, business was booming!

Matt was the sole occupant of the passenger section of the plane. Dan O'Malley was currently flying the Learjet under Bob Cummings's expert tutelage. Matt's thoughts dwelled on the past two days at the hunting lodge in British Columbia. He and Jeff Harrigan had witnessed the strange turn of events at the cabin. Satellite imagery had picked up all inside and outside activity. They had observed Frank Herrick's bid to dominate the other three and had heard most of the outside exchange and the plot to railroad Herrick. Then the startlingly vicious beating they gave him and their subsequent tying him to his bunk bed. *There was little doubt that Herrick would never rule THIS bunch!* The three had worked together making an early dinner, but ignored feeding any of it to Frank, although

Chester Bennett brought him a glass of water and an energy bar. What would happen the next day was anyone's guess, and Matt and Jeff were in agreement not to interfere. *These bastards deserve anything that gets handed to them.* Matt and Jeff agreed to abide by the instructions laid out regarding fighting. All rations would be cut in half for a month, and if any fighting broke out again, supplies would be cut again.

Bear had used one of their allotted SAT- NAV calls and left a message to have Herrick removed from their group. An hour later Jeff returned Bear's call and asked why,

"Because we beat the prick! He wanted to take over." Jeff's response was:

"You have not obeyed instructions. All supplies will be cut in half for the next month. If everyone gets along, normal delivery will take place the following month."

Bear started to argue, and that's when Jeff hung up. Bear related all this to the group, and they all reacted by cursing and yelling at Herrick

"This was all your fuckin' fault, you prick, and if you fuck with us again, you'll be beaten again."

But they sure as hell would hesitate calling again, for fear of further supply cuts.

Things calmed down a bit after that, and Matt and Jeff observed that each of the four men went quiet. Soon, the windup lamp was switched off, and quiet descended.

Matt was pleased that Jeff had matters well in hand, but did ask him if he needed another person to help out. His replied that he was comfortable with the arrangement, but promised to contact Matt immediately if things started to get tricky. They agreed to stay in touch, and would ensure the SAT-NAV phone was on 24/7.

Before showering in the aft section, Matt made a few calls and planned his New York visit. He showered, shaved, brushed his teeth and changed clothes. He prepared lunch for the three of them. He seldom travelled with stewardesses, as he preferred simplicity—as well as security—in all he said and did.

When lunch was ready, he carried the tray of food to the forward cabin. Opening the door, he set lunch down on a small fold-down table.

"Bob, you're not letting this clown drive, surely?"

They laughed, put the plane on autopilot and ate the delicious salad and ham croissants. Matt queried,

"Don, have you passed navigation yet? It feels that we're on our way to Hawaii."

—To which Don good-naturedly chided,

"I preferred the sun and surf of Hawaii to the smog of New York City and I hope you don't mind the small detour?"

They laughed again and levity turned to a more serious note, as Matt confided to them of the real purpose of the trip.

"Two more passengers will be captured and taken to the island. I hope you're game, because this involves a more complicated capture and could be on the dangerous side. Secrecy will be paramount, because the missing men already on the island are drawing attention in certain circles."

Bob and Dan were becoming intrigued with Matt's plan to make a difference in the world—and they too were starting to enjoy the chase.

"Who are you going after this time Matt?"

" I'll let you know, but not at this time. I will mention however, that of the two men, one will be extremely dangerous, while the other will produce serious political implications."

They were an hour away from John F. Kennedy International, and Bob took over from Dan. He started the pre-landing checks prior to descent. Matt left them to it and carried the empty tray to the plane's aft area. He cleaned up the dishes and ensured his bags were properly packed and his briefcase in order. It was going to be a busy week.

The landing was the smoothest landing that Matt had experienced in a long time, and for a change, they quickly arrived at their private hangar.

Charles Freemont was there to greet them and helped with the luggage. Greetings were exchanged and they proceeded to Charles's Mercedes, parked near the small hangar. They would rendezvous with the pilots: Cummings and O'Malley, again in forty-eight hours.

For as long he had known Charles, Matt had never known him to lose his cool, under any circumstance. He was the most professional man that he had ever met, aside from his father. He was absolutely solid, affable, organized and had an IQ that was off the charts. He even looked the part—wearing suits, shirts and ties from Gieves & Hawkes. They even supplied him with all the basics, such as shoes, socks, boxer shorts and all things leather. Charles dealt with them because of style, service and one-stop clothes shopping. He was too busy a man to look for fashion, and they provided his total wardrobe. He was handsome, elegant, and one of the fittest men that Matt had ever known. His good looks rivaled any movie star.

His Mercedes was far better equipped than any car on the market, plus he had bulletproof one-way glass installed to his specifications. He came from money but also made plenty of his own. Charles was vice president of West Coast operations, paid a handsome salary and also received shares in the company. Charles was well connected and treated everyone he met with extreme courtesy. Anyone who did a special favor for him would always receive a unique gift of appreciation. One individual had received a Rolex watch for supplying him with an important customer referral.

He had friendly, piercing blue eyes, a hawk nose, and a well-trimmed beard—he had his hair and beard trimmed daily, by a retired barber, in his office, while working on his computer. He had a ready smile, and his staff of twenty, were well taken care of. They loved working for him, and if things got a little critical, they stayed until the task was completed, sometimes well into the evening hours.

The office complex, located at 75 Rockefeller Tower in the Bevmax Office Tower, took up the entire 19th floor, with spectacular views of St. Patrick's Cathedral and Rockefeller Center. The tower complex had its own privately accessed parking area and elevator, which was entered by a security card. They rode up to the 19th floor and the elevator door opened to Space Security Watchers offices. They entered a small glass cubicle, but before the electronic door could be opened, both a handprint and voice imprint was required. A security guard was posted as a final security measure. No one was allowed in without being on his list. The guard scanned all who entered, before being buzzed into the main office area. These measures were necessary due to the nature of the security business.

Charles led the way through the offices and was greeted by everyone they passed. Satellite tracking monitors were manned 24/7. The sixty-inch monitors were impressive, showing crystal clear images of the varied businesses that contracted with them to monitor their operations. Charles was very proud to show Matt the revolutionary night monitoring systems. Charles and his staff had greatly improved the night focusing of the high quality cameras, and the clarity was truly amazing. This was one of the reasons for Matt's visit. Charles couldn't wait to show off his private new seventy-five inch monitor located in his office. Currently it was switched to a night shot of a London industrial complex which was so clear and precise, that when a parked white van was brought into sharp focus, the bolts holding the license plates could be seen, one of which required tightening!

Matt decided that changes were in order and this latest innovation would soon be implemented with the other branches. He readily complimented the beaming Charles. His dark walnut-paneled office was superb. The deep plush azure carpets reflected great taste, and his three desks were topped with thick ornate glass, supported by rare, rich Egyptian black and white veined marble bases. Lighting was dimmed at the present time, in order to ease eyestrain while watching the monitors. Each desk supported a monitor, and they could be switched to different locations by a touch of a key on the computers.

Matt was asked what locale was of interest to him and three came to mind. Only Charles's computer was able to access them. He performed his magic by hitting a special coded site on his computer. The changing to larger monitors was sheer genius! The eyestrain would be vastly reduced, and the bonus to the monitoring people was that the images they were looking at became clearer and more interesting.

They zeroed in on the island, they could see Chester and Bear having a conversation, and once Charles made a couple of keystrokes, their voices came through as clear as a bell. The two felons were currently talking about Frank Herrick, and the gist of their conversation pertained to: who the man was and where he came from. Herrick was quietly lying in his bunk. He'd finally been untied. Chester were saying,

"We'll leave him alone, but the minute the bastard tries anything, we'll throw him into the river and watch him drown. That way we won't be blamed, and our supplies wouldn't be cut."

The sound and the picture were cut, and Charles inquired if things on the island were progressing to Matt's satisfaction. Matt replied that they were, but admitted that his goal lacked only the final two malfactors: *Jack Mostar and the Right Honorable Allen T. Petrick.*

Charles was the only man privy to the entirety of the plan, and he was in complete support of what Matt was trying to achieve. He was also going to aid him in capturing the final two targets. On one of the monitors Charles brought up a video, taken earlier in the day by one of his investigators. The Judge Allen T. Petrick's home was of Tudor design, with numerous large windows and huge ornate double entrance doors. It had three floors, and its complicated roof surface included four brick chimneys and an unusual turret off to one side. The house was located on well-manicured lawns, amidst sculpted bushes and well-attended gardens. Snow had not yet made an appearance, and they could clearly see three fountains that had been shut off for winter. An iron fence ran around the entire property with thick shrubbery growing against it, which gave the property added security. A thick iron gate was the only access to the property—it was keypad operated. Antique lampposts were placed every ten feet all around the property.

Charles gave Matt his report regarding the whereabouts of the Petrick's family and servants. His wife was visiting some friends for the next several weeks in New Hampshire and a butler and cook lived in the basement of the house. The butler was currently on a week's vacation in Mexico. The judge and the elderly cook were the sole occupants living in the house, during the past week. Charles brought up a schematic of the house that including its antiquated security system, which could be deactivated temporarily, with a few keystrokes of their computers. The judge's computer calendar for the week was brought up on the monitor. The judge would be home every night for the next week, except for Saturday evening when he was to be picked up by three male colleagues—they would proceed to their men's club, for a night of poker. Matt made some notes and asked Charles to bring up the last person on the list.

Another video was brought up on the screen. Jack Mostar lived in a well-guarded downtown penthouse. A report showed that he was accompanied everywhere by three well-armed henchmen. When at home in his penthouse, a guard was stationed at the only door and was relieved 24/7 by one of the other two. The two were presently residing with Mostar, who wasn't straying far from his penthouse, due to the detaining of his boss, Gino Danelli. He was keeping a very low profile these days. Security of his penthouse was a touch keyboard and the access number was 009988. Matt didn't even bother to ask how this number combination had been obtained. Charles had remarkable talents, as well as excellent contacts. Matt made a few more notes and asked for a printout of the floor plans of both the Judge's house and Jack Mostar's penthouse apartment.

Their next stop was to check Matt into a secure hotel and then have dinner.

Chapter 18

"All rise! The court will now come to order. Judge Allen T Petrick presiding."

The side door to the courtroom opened, and a short stout man wearing black-rimmed glasses, a distinguished beard, and a black flowing robe entered through a private door leading from his chambers. He brusquely walked over to the high courtroom desk, hesitated, coldly surveyed the crowd, and sat down with a flourish. He poured himself some water from a glass pitcher and took his time drinking. He was not feeling entirely well. As a matter of fact, he was rather hung over from drinking an excessive amount of Balvenie, an eighteen-year-old single malt Scotch whisky, following a delicious late dinner, prepared by his elderly female cook. She was old, but was worth her weight in gold when it came to cooking, cleaning and general housekeeping duties. She knew how to shop too, and worked well within the food budget.

Thankfully, his wife was in New Hampshire, visiting with friends—he wished she would stay away forever. She never stopped talking. He could do nothing right, and she was forever nagging him about something.

Last night, after the cook went to bed in her basement room, he brought a bottle of scotch upstairs to his bedroom, shut and locked the door, entered the huge walk-in closet, reached up to the crown molding and pushed a small recessed button. The small enclosure was situated inside the turret of the house. To any outsider and the inhabitants of the mansion, it appeared to be only decorative. A door clicked open in the paneled wall, revealing a hidden six by eight foot room. Located on a small desk, rested his newest acquisition, a state-of-the-art fifty-four inch computer-tower.

An overhead shelf contained dozens of pornographic CDs, which he considered priceless.

Much of the collection was made possible by a recent bribe, paid to him, courtesy of Jack Mostar. He had never actually came face to face with the man, but one night, as he was having dinner at an exclusive restaurant, after having been served a delicious filet mignon, he was pondering which of the gourmet desserts to choose. As he was perusing the menu, a waiter brought over a bottle of Moet & Chandon, compliments of a beautiful lady dressed in a white evening gown. He tipped the waiter fifty dollars to approach the lady and ask her to join him. To his surprise and delight, she left her table and walked over to him, gave him a great smile and sat down opposite him. She was gorgeous! She had dark eyes, full lips and ample cleavage that the low-cut designer gown revealed in great detail.

"Before we get started," she said, "I just wanted to compliment you on your hobby."

Hobby? What hobby? Has she mistaken me for someone else?

"I uh—"

"By which I mean the collection of child pornography, of course," she said with a smile.

Petrick went pale. *How the fuck could this drop-dead gorgeous woman know about that?*

"I don't really know—"

"Do you think the world would enjoy hearing your little secret?" she asked, her voice sweet and measured.

Anything he was about to say caught in his throat.

"I don't know that most folks would understand. Luckily, this matter will remain between us, and you only have to agree to a ruling in our favor."

Dammit, I might have known. He found his voice then.

"Are you blackmailing a New York judge?"

She leaned in and lowered her voice slightly, her sultry facial expression betraying nothing of what she was saying.

"You're fucking right I'm blackmailing you! And here is the way it's going to happen. A ruling in your courtroom is coming down in a few months and I want you to rule in the defendants favor. Should you cooperate, you will receive a cash bonus of five hundred thousand dollars. Simple as that."

"And what ruling are we referring to?"

"The murder charge against Jack Mostar and his men."

"Are you outta your *fucking* mind?" he said, a cold sweat trickling down his back. "No one would believe it! It was out-and-out murder on their part. The District Attorney has an ironclad case! And everyone in New York knows it! Besides, I'm not even the presiding judge!"

People were starting to turn around, starting to stare.

"Lower your fucking voice right now," she said. "And start smiling!" She demonstrated with a smile of her own.

"Within the month, you'll replace the existing judge in the case!"

She sat back in her chair, and with a lovely smile, waited for his reply.

He managed to get himself under control, and, with one of his sincerest of smiles, leaned forward.

"I don't understand how and who will decide to make me the presiding judge."

"Don't sweat it judge, it WILL happen and you really don't have to know the how nor the who.

"And if I chose *not* to?"

"You're not listening," she said. "I already informed you what would happen, and make no mistake, it *will* happen!"

The judge slumped in his seat, defeated. The woman got up, reached over, patted him on the cheek, and left. Every eye in the restaurant watched her graceful exit.

The lady had been correct in all respects. The powers that be, replaced the current judge, who, conveniently had been videotaped with a well known local prostitute and had had the choice of going to trial or tender his resignation. He had chosen the latter.

The defense had chosen trial by Judge. That was the he first he actually saw the man in person. *Jack Mostar* and his three murderous thugs had all insolently stared at him throughout the trial. Judge Allen T Petrick knew in his heart that they were all guilty as sin and that he did not like these men at all. Particularly Jack Mostar. There was something about the man that made him quake inside. Although the man presented himself well and looked to be very successful and fit, there lurked an evilness of the vilest sort. The Judge was no stranger to evil men in his court, but none that could equal Jack Mostar. Within a week of the trial, Judge Petrick had managed to find a loophole in the case and declared a mistrial.

The courtroom erupted and the newspapers had a field day. The next evening, when he entered his car to drive to his home, he found a suitcase containing five hundred thousand dollars beside him on the front seat.

Last night, he'd turned on his home computer and inserted one of the child pornography CDs. There was an expensive cut glass snifter on the desk, and he poured himself two fingers of Balvenie, while he sat back and watched a splendid presentation on the exploitation of small children. To his delight, animals were involved. By the time he had emerged from his secret room, he was spent and very drunk.

He reluctantly turned his attention back to the goings-on in his court-room. A man convicted of beating a young boy—almost kicking him to death—was awaiting sentencing. The recovering youth would never be the same again. He had been in a coma for almost two weeks now and would probably never be able to walk again. The boy's parents and grandparents were in the first row, awaiting his verdict. Judge Allen Petrick read his notes, deliberated for a few moments and thought of the convicted man in front of him.

In all fairness to the accused, the boy had taunted the man relentlessly due to a speech impediment. The accused had a hair-lip and was a bad stutterer. So bad, in fact that he couldn't speak in his own defense—his lawyer had to speak on his behalf. The accused thirty-two-year-old man had simply lost his temper after a prolonged harangue from the boy, and, in a frenzy, had badly beaten the eight-year-old boy. *Where the hell were the boy's parents at the time? What was wrong with the little bastard, and why would he taunt a grown man? The kid was asking for it, and got what he deserved.*

He had the bailiff call the court to order and asked the accused to please rise. A hush fell on the packed courtroom.

"The verdict of this court is that the accused serve a one year suspended sentence doing community work. Court is dismissed!"

His courtroom erupted, as it had in the Mostar fiasco, everyone shouting and swearing about the unfair sentence. Judge Allen T. Petrick lost control of the courtroom at that point. He pounded his gavel for quiet, until it was broken. He ordered the bailiff to clear the court and to arrest anyone who didn't cooperate. A near riot would have taken place had the police not arrived to disperse the crowd. By then the judge had left the courtroom.

Matt was in the courtroom and had heard the verdict. He left the courtroom and joined Charles outside the Justice Department and climbed into Charles's Mercedes. Matt explained what had taken place.

"Welcome to the New York justice system," said Charles, "and Judge Allen T. Petrick. The man is simply a bad judge and a prick to boot. He fancies himself a god in his own mind. I'm going to enjoy helping you take this fellow down. He's a disgrace to the justice system and deserves what's about to happen to him!"

Judge Petrick was escorted out a side entrance of the Justice Department by three policemen and quickly climbed into his car and got the hell away from the madhouse. *What the fuck was wrong with those fucking people. They wanted to crucify the accused, for what? Reacting to the taunts of that vicious little eight-year-old boy?* The Judge could remember being bullied over and over again during his own boyhood years, and had grown ever so tired of it. If he had had a gun, he would have evened some scores.

And later during his law studies, he received more bullying of sorts. Some of the law students had resented him because of his outward appearance, his good grade scores, and, of course, the fact that he looked and acted like a nerd, didn't help his situation. He could remember some of the things that were done to him, like making him pee the bed by dipping one of his fingers in warm water, and taunting him mercilessly afterwards. Or the time they filled his Lexus with bags of garden soil. And the other time when they loaded his chili with extra hot peppers. He was sick for a week. Another time they photographed him while taking a shower and then posting dozens of those pictures all over the campus. Well the assholes weren't doing it now! *He* was now a court judge and no one fucked with a judge.

He drove directly to his residence, barricaded himself in his office, poured himself a stiff drink and sulked. He didn't even come out to eat his dinner. Later, he again carried a bottle of scotch up to his bedroom, slammed the door shut, locked it, and retreated into his pornographic little world.

It was one o'clock in the morning when Charles and Matt parked a rented van behind some shrubbery, a block from the Judge's home. While Charles waited in the van, Matt jogged to the back of the property, put on a pair of gloves, climbed over the high fence, and lay flat on the ground and surveyed the property. No dogs, no hidden alarms, no cameras or guards were in evidence. A friend of Charles, also in the security business, who owed him a few favors, had remotely disconnected the Judge's alarm.

Matt donned a ski mask, leather gloves and slowly approached a side door. Taking out his lock picks, he deftly picked the lock, and opened the well-oiled door and found himself inside a small garden foyer, containing gardening tools, pots, bags of soil and rainproof attire. He made his way through this maze and emerged into a corridor. The neat kitchen was located to his left, while the dining room was to the right. The table was set for one, and dinner was cold and untouched.

The next doorway led to a study, containing shelf after shelf of law books and first editions of well-known authors. The judge's desk was littered with stacks of legal files, note pads, and assorted writing implements. A near-empty bottle of scotch and an empty glass, occupied the desk. The last doorway led into a small sewing room, which was neat as a pin. He found a stairway that led to the basement area, while another back staircase led to the second-floor. He quietly climbed them and found himself in a corridor with all four doors closed, two on the right and two to the left. It was more or less the same layout as on the main floor. The first door he opened on his left was a spare bedroom, while the bedroom on the right was completely feminine. *Separate bedrooms perhaps?* Proceeding to the next door, he cautiously turned the doorknob and found it locked.

Matt looked up and down the dim corridor, knelt down, took out his lock pick and quietly set to work. Within a minute the door lock yielded to his efforts and he cautiously opened it. Matt observed a king size four-poster bed and two large easy chairs to the left of the bed. The bed was turned down, but devoid of anyone in it. The en suite bathroom was also empty.

Where the hell is he? Matt was considering a continued search of the house, when he heard faint snoring sounds. He followed the sound to the large masculine walk-in closet and observed an open door leading into a small room. The judge was passed out in his chair. He appeared to be dead drunk. In front of him was a large monitor showing a lured picture of some sort of child pornography, in great detail and clarity. Matt wondered what disgusted him more: the pornography or the judge—of all people—watching it.

Charles was waiting for Matt's call and told to wait five minutes while Matt looked for the mechanism that opened the main gate. Charles drove through the opening and it reclosed behind him. Matt signaled him to enter through the front door and Charles was soon at his side. Matt quietly led him up the stairs and whispered in his ear that he had something strange to show him. Curious as to what this might be, they entered the judge's bedroom and followed Matt into the tiny room. There he saw the passed out form of Judge Allen T. Petrick—and what the man had been watching when he had passed out.

What more could be said? Matt drew his dart gun and shot the man in the side of the neck. Petrick emitted only a small grunting sound. They lifted him off the chair and carried him to his en suite and shaved off his beard. He would be harder to recognize that way and where they were taking him, it was probably best if he wasn't recognized.

The plan was to leave the computer on, showing the contents of the small turreted room, and leave the panel open. The door to the bedroom was relocked. The locked door would alarm the person who would eventually come looking for the judge, and someone would have to break it down and go looking for him. They picked up the inert judge and carried him out to the van. They drove through the gate and it automatically re-closed and they slowly drove away.

They arrived at the airport at two thirty in the morning and drove directly to the Learjet, parked and carried the sleeping judge inside the plane, handcuffing him to the hidden cot and slid the panel back into place. *One down and one to go*, Matt thought.

"I wonder who will break into his bedroom?"

They both agreed that it wouldn't be the elderly housekeeper because she didn't have the strength to do so—she would probably call a neighbor or the police.

Both men smiled grimly at what the police would find. There would be some type of public outrage, and with the judge's reputation, the outcry would be loud! Charles was concerned about the reaction of Petrick's wife but Matt was of the opinion that she would probably be relieved to be rid of him, as he probably was a miserable bastard to live with anyway. Charles had to admit that he was enjoying this latest adventure.

"How do you think the judge will do on the island?" asked Charles. "Not his usual crowd I daresay."

"My guess is that he is about to see what life really is about without a silver spoon in his mouth. He's likely to learn some unpleasant truths about himself."

Conversation turned to their final challenge: *the capture of Jack Mostar.*

Chapter 19

The cabin's early-morning silence was shattered by Frank Herrick's scream. He was having a nightmare. Paris prostitutes whom he had beaten over the years were haunting his dreams, beating him with baseball bats, golf clubs and broom handles. Bear woke him by throwing a boot at his head, and he awoke sweating and wondering where he was. The three men yelled at him to shut the fuck up. It was now four in the morning, and the three of them couldn't get back to sleep. Herrick, however, returned to his dreams, and once more, his screams startled everyone again and this time Bear picked up his other boot, strode over to Herrick's lower bunk, and started beating on him with it. Frank Herrick was getting beaten in his nightmare, and now Bear was whacking him with his boot.

Jazz and Chester, who were, by now, thoroughly pissed, picked Herrick up and bodily threw him out into the cold, barring the door after him.

Herrick found himself out in the freezing cold, clad only in his pants and shirt. His bare feet were already starting to freeze, and his teeth started to chatter. He thought back to when he had kicked Jazz out into the same cold conditions. He also knew that no one would come to his aid, for they had, by now, banded together because of his initial attempt at trying to control the group. What a mistake *that* had been! These were assholes that no one dare tamper with. Frank Herrick was in a bad way. The group of three inside the cabin chose not to even include him in the meals they prepared. So far, he only subsisted on water and health bars. He was growing weaker by the hour. They also forced him to do *more* than his share of the chores. They didn't trust him with the axe however, so they split the wood themselves, and Jazz slept with the axe to avoid Herrick getting his hands on it.

He finally walked to the door and shouted at them to let him in because he was freezing. Silence greeted him for a few moments, and that was when Jazz shouted through the door.

"We'll let you in when you beg, you *prick!*"

Frank had little choice, and for the first time in his life, he begged. Something seemed to break inside him at that moment, and he would never again be the same.

They opened the door, and he hastily entered and stood next to the stove for warmth. The trio of men simply stared at him. He did not see any pity in them, only their cruel unforgiving stares. He went to his bunk, got into his sleeping bag and tried to get warm—afraid to sleep, lest he fall back into his nightmare state. Frank Herrick was starting to feel ill. He was sweating profusely. This was followed by the shakes and he was having trouble breathing—soon he was fighting for air.

The trio made food for themselves, and the smell of coffee soon permeated the cabin. They made little attempt at conversation, each lost in their own private thoughts.

Jazz was thinking of his home turf and how fast he was losing control of his old life. He knew his followers were by now drifting to other gangs, as they were just too stupid to make it on their own. The only person who would miss him was an aging aunt. He had frequently helped her by bringing her groceries, and she had grown to rely on him. He was surprised with himself that he was missing her and wondering how she was doing without him. He also found that he didn't altogether hate it here and was tolerating the strange camaraderie of Bear and Chester Bennett. He had never experienced quiet and peacefulness in his life and found himself *not missing* the cruelty and harshness of the big city.

Bear was thinking of missed opportunities in the crime world as he sat on this fuckin' island in the middle of goddamn nowhere! He was finding that Jazz, as stupid as a bad wet dream, had a nice side to him too—he found himself starting to like the little creep. Chester however was another story. He kept to himself and was cooperative in helping in the preparation of the meals and did his share of chores, but he never talked about where he came from or what he did for a living. Bear would never trust the man —there was just something about him that Bear couldn't put his finger on.

Chester was just plain terrified that the mob would somehow chase him down and kill him because he had left them high and dry. He was still completely mystified as to who was responsible for his being at this God forsaken hell on earth. He longed to obtain the axe from Jazz so he could chop up that Herrick bastard!

As the weather had warmed a bit, the trio decided to explore the island and start looking for another way to escape. They dressed and left the cabin together without so much as a second glance toward Herrick. The day was bright and sunny for a change. The trio noticed that the cabin was situated high on the island and invisible to anyone traveling the river. The cabin was in a bit of a clearing, protecting it from the elements. Steep cliffs were located along both sides of the island and were too steep to climb, up or down.

At the top end, a steep path descended to the river and evened out to a flat spot, about the size of a small house. The river flowed on either side of the point, and the view was a stimulating one. The river was wild and scary, and it would be dangerous to try and launch any type of craft, due to the current and sharp rocks that stuck up everywhere.

They climbed the path back up to the cabin and proceeded to the lower end of the island, where the river was less fearsome. They passed the spot where the huge spruce—the one they had all been tied to—was located. Again, a faint path led down to the river. This was the spot, in all probability, where the boat that brought them here, had beached. Land was barely discernible, and any attempt to swim it would be impossible. Besides, no one in the trio could swim to begin with. They rested on some flat boulders and attempted to plan an escape. The choices were few, and though they explored the few possibilities, they came up short of any ideas.

Back in the cabin, Frank Herrick was starting to hallucinate. He was gasping for breath, and any movement resulted in severe pain. He was burning up with fever and had neither the stamina nor the will to stop what he knew was going to happen to him. He was dying, and he was doing it alone. He was too weak even to call out. His life flashed in front of his eyes, and he remembered all the evil he had caused. He remembered the countless murders he had ordered done by his men and the cruelty they inflicted on their victims. Frank remembered killing his parents with the baseball bat and the satisfaction it had once given him. The memories of the hurt and the killing of all those Paris prostitutes haunted him too. Frank Herrick, at that point, wished he could make amends and start all over again. Every memory filled him with regret. His life was starting to drain away, and all was starting to fade. The last thing he saw before dying, was the bright sunlight, flowing through the front window of the cabin.

At midday the trio returned to the cabin, added more wood to the stove and started making preparations for their next meal. Jazz decided to rouse Herrick to help him with chores. He kicked the bunk, but there was no movement. He bent down and found himself looking at a dead man, and leapt back.

"What the *fuck*!?"

Bear and Chester approached the dead man and took turns prodding him. They realized that they were the ones responsible for the Frank Herrick's demise and retreated to the table and sat down. Silence ensued. They were all a little stunned, but these men were not strangers to death, and they also knew that they had a dicey matter on their hands. Strangely enough, all agreed that the solution was not to throw him into the river. Instead they decided to find a spot, and bury him.

They decided to find a suitable place for burial. They chose the head of the river, in the flat spot, because the proximity of the river which had caused the earth to soften somewhat. Jazz and Chester took turns digging a grave, using the two shovels and the axe. Bear took his turn and finished the digging. He felt a cold shiver go through him, and wondered why? It took them two and a half hours to finish. They stopped at five feet because they ran into too much water and returned to the cabin, and, leaving the body in the now zipped up sleeping bag, carried it down to the grave and slowly lowered it into the ground. Turns were taken shoveling the dirt and gravel back into the grave. Not a word had been spoken while this took place and Bear was the one who finally asked if anyone wanted to say any last words. No one volunteered, and the final gesture, was lifting a heavy rock and placing it in the middle of the mounded earth. Once more the captives filed back up the incline and reentered the cabin. The trio didn't eat that night, as their appetites had died with Frank Herrick.

Jeff kept Matt apprised of all this by SAT phone and both men were saddened by the quick death of Frank Herrick. This is something they had failed to plan for, but decided that little was to be done about it and concluded that the trio couldn't have handled the situation any better. This was the end to an evil man. The world would not mourn him.

Matt relayed the news to Charles, explaining everything that had led up to the demise of Frank Herrick. Charles couldn't get over the fact that so much had happened within a two-week period. It has certainly saved the legal system a lot of money. He also wondered if any more of the remaining island prisoners would meet their end on the island. Matt wondered the same thing, but present plans wouldn't be changed, except that now there was an extra vacancy to be filled, and he was confident he would soon find a replacement!

Chapter 20

While Barney Satch was away for the day, setting up new bank accounts for his sister, Nina decided to take advantage of his absence and catch up on some long overdue computer work. Sara was currently helping Jeremy with some in-home school activity in the TV room. Nina was sitting at the kitchen table reviewing her emails when she ran across one from Jessica Rawlins, a girlfriend she had known all her life.

EXTREMELY URGENT – Nina, I need your help! As you know I am head-researcher for Melcan Pharmaceuticals in Dallas, which, up to now is a company I love working for. You are aware that my life has been dedicated to product research. I have recently run into a very dangerous situation. A product called Wartavan is being developed and is still in the test stage. The product is being introduced to combat obesity in children and is currently being tested on thirty-six laboratory rats which have been fed foods that make them overweight.

Then Wartavan was injected into them for one month at the rate of two injections per day. During this time period, they had the choice of eating either the unhealthy diet or normal healthy food. In every case, they chose the healthy diet and completely ignored the junk food. All of the rats lost their excess weight very quickly! It was deemed a success.

Due to the number of obese children that are prevalent in America, Melcan couldn't wait to market this new drug.

But then, a strange thing happened: eight of the rats died two days after the test was completed. Naturally, the eight dead rats were immediately autopsied by two of the researchers and the cause was a simple one. In each case the rats died because of a low red cell count. We concluded that the drug was deemed too dangerous and our recommendation was to cease all production and all subsequent marketing. The power-that-be, namely Zachery Melcan himself, has chosen, for reasons only known by him, to proceed with it.

Then I happened to come across a memo on his desk; he was attempting to contact a particular lobbyist, who happens to be on vacation for the next two weeks. Zachery is prepared to pay the lobbyist a large amount of money to ram the drug through and obtain government approval.

The next day, when the two researchers in question, didn't show up for work, I became alarmed and tried to contact them, but all I got was their answering machines. I then discovered that the lab rat autopsy reports were missing too. Midmorning of the same day, a sheriff and his deputy paid me a visit. I learned that one of the researchers, on her way to her apartment, had been killed when a truck struck her car at an intersection. The truck left the scene and disappeared.

I was also informed that the second researcher had turned up dead in an alley due to an overdose of heroin. She was found with a syringe still stuck in her arm! Naturally, the sheriff department became suspicious---that two people in the same day, working for the same company, was just too coincidental. I was horrified by this news and informed the official that now I was frightened for my own life. They asked me if there was a secure place I could stay at for the remainder of the investigation? I told them that I had an aunt who lived just outside of Dallas. They advised me not to use my credit card for the next while, as any purchases could be easily tracked--- and to withdraw some cash from a nearby bank machine. They then drove me to my aunts home, took my phone number and asked me to stay put until I heard from them again.

Nina, I'm so scared! I am also frightened that should Wartavan be approved, many children could die! I don't know which way to turn. I'm asking you for advice. Please, please help me. I have no one else to turn to. I have my laptop with me. Email me back. Jessica

Nina was both alarmed and disturbed by her friend's email, and after some thought, phoned Matt on his SAT phone. He picked up and Nina briefly summarized the situation. When she finished, Matt was quiet for a full minute, before he replied.

"First of all, would you mind forwarding the email to my secure email address? Secondly, find out all you can on this Zachery character. Thirdly, I think Jessica would be well advised to keep a very low profile, until we get to the bottom of this mess. I'm as concerned as you are that the bastard might just get this drug approved. I know the game they play and should they get the right lobbyist, with enough funds backing him up, it probably *will* go through. In the meantime, I'll have my investigators do some digging. This guy has to be stopped one way or the other, or a lot of children could die. We obviously don't have a lot of time to act. Let's get to work."

Matt knew of two investigators in Dallas on whom he could count on and when he talked to them, they immediately went into action and would report to him as soon as they came up with anything on Zachery Melcan.

Nina was concentrating all her efforts on her computer and was arriving at some interesting revelations. She found that Melcan Pharmaceuticals was currently experiencing financial difficulty and was in dire need of capital. She also found out that this was not the first time this had happened. She brought up Zachery Melcan's profile and found him to be an elegant forty-six year old, born into money and well connected. He sported a mustache; an engaging smile, intense blue eyes, tailored suits, and wore bow ties. His wife had left him long ago and he was currently without companionship. Nina's overall impression was that he liked high fast living and liked to dominate. Personally, she found him repugnant—although she realized that she might be influenced by Jessica's current situation. She hacked into his personal bank account and found only a small balance. The corporate account did not have a healthy balance either, and when she dug a little deeper, found that Melcan was in the habit of withdrawing huge amounts of cash—usually in the half million-dollar range—about every two or three months without being replaced. The company's bank account was incurring large hits and she could easily see that they were in trouble. Her first guess, in regards to the withdrawals, was due to bribes to various lobbyists or government officials.

Matt's investigators were quick to trace Zachery Melcan's latest travel itinerary. By accessing his Corporate American Express statements, they found that he frequently travelled to Las Vegas and Atlanta and always stayed at the finest hotels. In Las Vegas, it was always The Bellagio and in Atlanta, The Ritz-Carlton. He usually arrived Friday and returned to Dallas Sunday evening. They contacted an agency in Las Vegas, and it was quickly established that Melcan was a big gambler. He favored baccarat and craps, and was a heavy loser.

He was currently into the casinos for over a million dollars, and they were starting to exert pressure on him to pay up. The answers were starting to come very quickly now and they soon came up with the obvious reasons.

He had to come up with a real winner in order to pay off his gambling debts, meaning that he had to quickly get the Wartavan drug on the market, regardless of a few lives. *This was one evil bastard!*

While sitting with Charles, Matt received the reports from Nina and the Dallas investigators. He asked that they keep close tabs on Zachery Melcan's whereabouts. He now had all he required to put together an accurate picture on Zachery the man. He and Charles concluded that the man had to be quickly isolated and both concluded that they now had their next island candidate.

But right now they had to deal with the whereabouts of Jack Mostar. He had dropped out of sight and they were having trouble locating him. Mostar was a savvy character that seemed to have a sixth sense when it came to survival. Time was running out and Matt was pondering what to do next. Charles came up with a solution. Why not skip Mostar for now and fly instead to Dallas, capture Zachery Melcan, and fly directly to the island. Matt liked the suggestion and phoned his pilots to ready the Learjet, informing them of the new flight plan.

Charles drove Matt to the airport and promised to keep in close touch, confident that he could pull all the stops and locate Mostar. The Learjet took off for Dallas an hour later.

Chapter 21

Zachery Melcan emerged from his Lexus LS600HL, glanced nervously in both directions and thought he noticed an unusual movement—a man who had perhaps too hastily turned to look into a shop window. He knew that the Las Vegas and Atlanta casinos wanted to collect the money owed to them. He knew he was way past due and that they did not play games. *Ironic when you think about it.* He had asked them for a thirty-day grace period—he was waiting for his latest drug to be approved and one of the casinos wanted a percentage of the profits from his company. No way they would receive a percentage, as it would be in the millions! He did negotiate some interest on the amount owed. They had settled on twenty percent, but only on the condition that his debt and interest be paid within thirty days.

When he entered Melcan Pharmaceuticals, he passed his security desk and the guard waved hello. Zachery thought this would be a good time to make a surprise visit to all departments. The current number of staff exceeded two hundred and forty; working in ten departments: Security, Product Development, Research, Marketing & Promotion, Manufacturing & Inspection, Procurement & Materials Import, Receiving, Shipping, Printing & Package Assembly and finally, General Office Staff & Staff development.

He was generally pleased after meeting with all department heads, save one. The research lab was currently void of people. His final stop was his fifth floor office area. He greeted his lovely secretary, entered his office and carefully glanced down to street level to see if the suspicious man was still in the area. The street was empty. *Christ, I am getting more paranoid by the day!*

He sat behind his desk and reviewed his messages. *Shit, that asshole lobbyist has yet to contact me.* He checked his emails and found nothing of interest. He organized his desk for the day ahead, called his secretary to bring in some coffee and join him for a few minutes. Evelyn Twain was a looker and had brains to match. He also knew she was attracted to him. She certainly knew how to make an entrance, even while carrying coffee. The coffee was fresh, and her company welcome. She had been hired the year previous and had come highly recommended. Evelyn sat across from him and crossed her legs. He loved those legs. *My God, if only she wasn't wearing panties!* He could visualize her sitting there in the nude!

He abruptly brought himself back to the business at hand. He inquired if all had run smoothly while he was away on another gambling trip. He reflected on another failed gambling spree.

Evelyn informed him of the sheriff's visit to Jessica Rawlins and her being escorted out of the building. *Fuck, she was next on my hit list as I had arranged with the two men who usually did this type of work for me. They were expensive, but very professional. Jessica Rawlins was due to be taken out within the week!* Zachery wasn't concerned at all about what her arrest would mean to him. After all, he had an ironclad alibi; two of the researchers had been taken care of and most importantly, the Wartavan follow-up report had been destroyed.

He wondered if Jessica had been arrested for the suspected killings? After all, she was the head of the department. A seed of an idea was forming in his head as to how he could implicate her in the murders. He made a note to himself to do so the following morning. Zachery had done similar things over the years, and he was no stranger on how to play the game. The hit squad he used to remove troublesome meddlers in the past had met similar fates. He also eliminated some of his competitors by using the same people.

Disposal was never done cheaply, but in the long run it certainly paid off. Gambling had always been his downfall. It drove his wife and children from him, and his relationship with his parents had greatly suffered. They no longer helped him in paying off his debts and had stopped talking to him long ago

Zachery asked Evelyn if there were any further concerns.

"What should we do about the Product Development Department— now that the department has three missing people?"

"Unless these people fail to reappear by tomorrow, we should promote one of the people in production to head up research and possibly one more person I have in mind to fill in as assistant. Please arrange Personnel to come up with two additional replacements?"

There were no other issues for the moment and Evelyn was free to go. She scooped up the empty coffee cups and walked to the outer office. His eyes followed her until she disappeared from view. He shook his head. He had a busy day ahead of him. His mind drifted back to the man looking into the shop window, and he felt uneasy all over again.

His concentration on work became so intense that, when he finally looked up, the sun was starting to set. He stretched, and walked to the outer office. All the staff had left for the day except for Evelyn, who was just finishing up. She looked so good sitting there, that he impulsively asked her if she would like to have a drink with him—and perhaps order in some dinner. He held his breath.

"I would love to," she replied.

They withdrew into his office and went to the small bar area. He asked her what she would like to drink, and she asked him if he had any champagne. He reached into the bar fridge and withdrew a bottle of Dom Pérignon Rose 2002, positioning it in a wine bucket filled with ice. He withdrew two chilled goblets from the freezer compartment and set them on the counter and with a flourish, popped the cork, filled their glasses, and proceeded to toast one another. They were both a bit hungry. A can of imported caviar and crackers was served up by Zachery and they ate while sitting on barstools. When the second glass was poured, Evelyn informed him that anything beyond a second would make her quite tipsy. They toasted again, drained the glasses, and a third was poured. Evelyn excused herself to use the bathroom.

A few minutes later, she emerged, dressed only in her high heels and very brief panties. Zachery Melcan was speechless. She walked over to him and whispered in his ear, how, from the day she first met him, she had wanted to remove his ever-present bow tie along with the rest of his clothing. She ordered him not to move until she had completely disrobed him.

At four in the morning, Zachery phoned security to call a taxi for Evelyn, as she was in no condition to drive. A second bottle of Champagne had been opened and they had become quite giddy and deliciously uninhibited! They were now dressed—his bow tie once again in place—he escorted the giddy, giggly Evelyn Twain down to the waiting taxi. She truly couldn't handle more than her allotment of two drinks! Once she was seated inside the cab, he leaned inside the cab and gave her a deep lingering goodnight kiss. While doing so, he felt her put something into his pants pocket. He paid the driver a hundred dollars to ensure she was escorted safely up to her apartment. Zachery walked to his executive parking space and climbed into his Lexus. He was famished and drove to a nearby twenty-four hour restaurant for much needed sustenance. He didn't notice the dark rental van that followed him.

As he was waiting for a breakfast of steak and eggs, his thoughts drifted back to his night of frivolity. He couldn't stop thinking of the earth-shattering sex he'd had with Evelyn. He had to see her again! It was all he could think of. So engrossed was he in his sweet recollection that he barely remembered eating the delicious meal.

He hurriedly paid his waitress and returned to his car, which was parked beside a dark Chrysler van. When he climbed into his car, he failed to notice the man sitting directly behind his seat and as he was reaching for the button to start the Lexus, he heard a hissing sound and a stinging sensation to his neck, then all slowly faded to blackness.

Chapter 22

What the hell have I gotten myself into?

Charles Freemont was stumped, and this was not something he was used to. He was starting to realize that Jack Mostar was nobody's fool. The man seemed to have a sixth sense about danger, and had the instincts of a cat. Charles too, was a survivor, and had good instincts of his own. He put himself in Mostar's shoes. It was evident that Mostar enjoyed luxury, ate in the finest restaurants, loved to be in the company of beautiful women, enjoyed the Arts and always surrounded himself within professional henchmen. Charles put himself into a more creative mode, sat at his desk and made some notes:

- Surveillance of his Central Park penthouse
- Where were Mostar and his henchmen?
- Access his driver's license for picture identification
- Track him through American Express or Visa
- was he using an alias? Check restaurants and theaters
- where would he likely set up temporary residence?
- Was he running?
- Check airports

Charles called for his security team and a resident computer expert to meet in his office. Five men and one woman joined him. Without going into specific detail, he told them he was tracking someone very elusive, crafty and dangerous. He also informed them to keep this matter top priority and completely confidential. The name of the man was given to each member as they were assigned a task. They were to begin immediately and drop what they were doing for the next twenty-four hours.

Three hours later, information began to trickle in. Mostar's whereabouts was tracked via American Express. He had used it to purchase air tickets to Seattle yesterday morning. He was presently checked into the Fairmont Olympic Hotel in downtown Seattle.

Charles relayed this news to Matt, who was now in mid-flight to his hunting lodge, and both agreed that Jack Mostar was there on business. It was obvious that he was sniffing around Gino Danelli's territory. Matt ordered immediate surveillance on Danelli's villa. Now that they had located him, they didn't want to lose him again. Matt's investigators would track his ground movements and as soon as he vacated his hotel, his room would be bugged and telephones tapped.

—

Jack Mostar and his three henchmen had breakfast delivered to their room, as they wanted to maintain a low profile. Following breakfast, he spoke to his men.

"This trip could payoff big-time, and if we play our cards right, we could take over Danelli's territory. But we have to tread carefully, so I'll outline what I have in mind. The Feds are likely to be watching us. I want two of you to leave the hotel separately and steal two cars, then drive them a few blocks from here. When this is done, phone me on my throw away phone, and tell me where you're parked. I'll give you the number before you leave. We'll all leave dressed casually, but no sunglasses or hats! Use different exits when you leave the hotel at five-minute intervals. We'll meet at Danelli's villa. I'll go in alone and speak to his wife. We'll want a very low profile while we're there, so stay in the cars and stay *real* alert!"

—

Louisa Danelli was a wreck and wasn't sure what to do. Three days prior, she had received a call from Gino, who briefly told her of his situation. The FBI had granted him only two phone calls, the first to his lawyer and the second to her—on vacation with her parents in Italy. When she heard that he was in FBI custody, she had nearly fainted. He asked that she return home immediately. He couldn't give much detail, other than to mention that someone had completely drained the bank accounts and that he was being held without bail. Prior to saying goodbye, he asked her not to tell the children anything and to give them a hug for him.

When she and the children arrived at the villa, no one was there to greet them. No guards, no servants and no Gino. She let herself into the empty home and had the children go to bed, for it had been a long and tiring trip. The plane from Madrid had been delayed three hours; due to mechanical difficulties, and to top it all off, deplaning took an hour extra, because of a faulty door. Louisa tried to sleep, but finally gave up to wander the villa. She finally laid down on a couch in Dino's study, managed to get a couple of hours sleep and woke up feeling tired and exhausted. She had tried for two days to find out where her husband was being held but to no avail. She phoned Gino's lawyer, but he was not in and wasn't expected back for the remainder of the week. Just as she hung up, the front doorbell chimed and when she rushed to open the door, a man she did not recognize was standing there.

Jack Mostar introduced himself, informing her of his association with her husband. She recognized his name and invited him inside. Louisa was a remarkable looking woman—*easy on the eyes*. She had a proud, patrician face and full-lipped smile. Her clear azure eyes held his gaze while they talked. He liked the way she took care of herself and guessed that she probably worked out regularly at a local gym. She asked him if he wanted an espresso? He gratefully accepted and while he waited in the living room, she left to fetch the beverage. Jack had never been in Gino's house, but he liked what he saw. The villa was his kind of place! Louisa brought a tray of the fragrant refreshment and sat in a chair across from him.

"I'm as shocked as you are about Gino," Jack said, "and I flew here as soon as I was able. Have you talked with Gino at all?"

"He phoned me in Italy. The children and I were visiting my parents at the time. Naturally, he didn't go into great detail, as he was in FBI custody. I've been trying to locate him for two days, but the authorities are stonewalling me. When I tried phoning his lawyer, I was told that he was unavailable for the rest of the week. Our bank accounts have been cleaned out, by someone. That's all that I know for sure."

Mostar said, "My sources tell me that both Gino and Bruno Cesare were picked up from here. Gino's men are confused, and everything is in disarray because no one is around to keep things organized, plus, their funds are diminishing, and we both know what *that* means."

"Do you have any suggestions on what can be done?"

Jack smiled inwardly to himself. *Oh, I have suggestions all right.*

"First of all, I assume you require funds with which to operate. I can transfer funds to cover this from our Eastern operations. But I will require the names of the men who work for Gino. Do you have access to these names?"

Louisa grew cautious.

"I have a safety deposit box at a nearby bank listing all the names, addresses and phone numbers of all his contacts. He had this all updated before I left for Italy. Dino is a very careful man and his complete operation is detailed inside a ledger. However, I would have to ask his permission to reveal its contents. The FBI do not know that I have an account under my maiden name."

Jack Mostar was so close, but he badly needed to convince her to give him the gang members contact information.

"I completely understand your dilemma in handing over this ledger. I only came here to help, due to my respect for Dino and if you are not comfortable in all this, I'll return to New York. Timing, however, is crucial to all our survival and the time to act is short. Perhaps you have an alternate plan I can help you with?"

"I cannot give you the ledger without my husband's consent, but I can and will give you the name of his men and how to contact them. As to the remaining information, I must wait to obtain his permission."

Mostar was more than happy to receive this information, for he had little doubt that he could elicit everything he required from Dino's men.

"I think you are wise in your decision. At least we will be able to keep things from falling apart. To start the ball rolling, I will transfer one hundred thousand dollars into your account. It is, after all, Dino's money."

Louisa was both happy and relieved to have made a worthwhile decision and immediately left the room to obtain her safety deposit box key. She reentered and said,

"When I obtain this information, "how will I get it to you?"

"Why don't I drive you there now?"

"I would do so, but I have no one to watch my children."

"Why not bring them with us, and we'll drive directly to the bank? Is it far?"

"That would work. Let me get the children ready."

Jack could barely suppress a smile. *It was starting to come together!*

—

Matt's plane had just landed when he received Charles's call.

"Sorry to bother you Matt, but I have news that couldn't wait."

"You located him, didn't you?"

"The bastard is clever. He eluded us somehow, but your idea of surveillance on Dino's villa paid off. He arrived there in one of two cars. He walked unaccompanied to the front door and rang the doorbell. For the past half hour, he's been inside, presumably with Danelli's wife. She and her two children flew in three days ago, according to my sources."

"See if you can get a license plate on his cars. We don't want to lose him again, plus, if I make it over there quickly, maybe we'll be lucky enough to nail the bastard on our own turf."

"Hang on, he's coming out of the house. A woman and two kids are accompanying him to his car. Wonder what the hell that's all about?"

"Can you have them followed?" Matt asked.

"Already happening. We've now got the license number of both cars. Don't hang-up; maybe they're not going far. I'm in contact as we speak."

Hang on! Both cars appear to be turning into a nearby shopping mall. The woman is getting out and entering a bank."

"I doubt if she'll be making a withdrawal. I'll bet she's getting something from her safety deposit box. Could be she is going to give Mostar information regarding the organization?"

It took the woman thirty minutes before she exited the bank carrying a large envelope and reentered the car.

"She was a long time in the bank," Charles said. "I wonder why."

"Maybe she had the bank photocopy part of whatever she had stored there. I'd love to see what it was."

"Matt, I've just learned that their hotel room is now wired for sound, with a video feed. The phones have also been bugged. Maybe we can do a little listening in when they return to the hotel."

"I have to leave you for now, Charles. But please phone me with an update as soon as you hear anything."

—

Louisa and the children were driven back to the villa, and Mostar escorted them back inside. He informed Louisa that, while she was in the bank, he had one hundred thousand dollars transferred to her account. He asked her to verify this with her bank. She went to make the call. She verified that the transaction had taken place, and greatly relieved. Without any further hesitation, she handed Jack Mostar the envelope containing photocopies her husband's gang-member contact information. He was a happy man and shook hands with Louisa before he departed.

The two cars returned to the hotel and Jack started phoning the gang-members. His first four calls went unanswered, and he chose not to leave any messages. On the fifth try, a gruff sounding man, who wanted to know *who the fuck was calling*, answered. Jack was careful in choosing the right words.

"My name is Jack Mostar, and I run the Eastern Division for Gino Danelli. Have you heard of me?"

"I don't fuckin' know anyone by dose names!"

"Whom am I talking to?"

"I go by the name of Alf and that's all you have to fuckin know for now!"

"I want you to ask around as to who I am. When you do, phone me back on the number I'm going to give you. I know all about what has happened to Danelli, and I'm here to help keep things organized until his release. I'm sure one of you has met me and know who I am. If you're at all interested, I'll be sitting at Luigi's restaurant on 6th and 4th tonight at eight, in a private room at the back of the restaurant. I suggest that no more than three of you show up. Anymore would arouse suspicion."

He could almost hear the Alf's gears turning as he spoke.

"I'll ask around," he said and hung up.

Well, it's a start. In anticipation of the meeting, Jack phoned Luigi's to make a reservation for four. Two of his men would be sitting in the main dining area. He sat at the hotel and started planning the evening meeting and kept his fingers crossed.

—

Charles again called Matt using his SAT phone.

"You called at a good time. I've just had a late lunch, and later tonight, we're installing the island's two latest inhabitants. So, what are the latest happenings in Seattle, Charles?"

"Mostar made a contact and has called for a meeting tonight, but only indicated that he would meet with three representatives from the gang. He can verify the three by checking their names from the list that Louisa Danelli gave him. I've already arranged to have a listening device in the backroom of the restaurant. A video would be impossible to install though. To answer your concern as to how long he'll be in Seattle, I'd estimate it would take him at least three days to get things organized there, so you probably have time to come and get him if you hurry."

"Charles, can you imagine the confusion when Mostar disappears?"

Charles was enjoying Matt's exhilaration and was starting to enjoy the island process and asked Matt if he could accompany him on the next island visit. Matt replied by saying he would look forward to his company and said he would be back in Seattle within twenty-four hours. Charles would fly to Seattle from New York via one of their corporate jets and join him there.

—

Jack Mostar was nervous as he waited for the three men to join him at Luigi's. It was now seven fifty-five. They weren't going to be early, by any means. The seconds slipped by, and a waiter appeared by his side, bent to ear level and introduced himself as Sean Mallory and he admitted that he wanted to meet Jack up close, one on one.

"I've met you briefly when I accompanied Gino Danelli to New York, when he first hired you. Mind if I sit down?"

Jack did remember him and was astounded that Sean had selected this simple method of making. He was also surprised at the man himself. He even resembled a waiter. He was unassuming, had average looks and no distinguishing marks. He was serious and direct.

"Sit down, would you like a drink?"

"Only coffee, thank you."

"Will anyone else be joining us"?

"Two gentlemen will be joining us as soon as coffee is served, which is their signal that everything is on the up and up."

"I applaud your caution."

Sean sat back while coffee was served, and two unassuming men entered the room and joined them. They introduced themselves as Craig and Sid and both ordered coffee. Jack asked the waitress to shut the door and give them an hour's privacy. He tipped her with a hundred dollar bill before she departed.

"Have any of you heard from Gino or Bruno?" asked Jack.

"Not a word," said Sean. "The Feds are really keeping a lid on everything. We have been unable to obtain a thing. Everything's a mess and we badly need to get something going or everything will fall apart."

This was the news Jack had been waiting for. The time to act was now. He hit them with a simple plan.

"I think we should meet quickly. Is there any objection to a meeting at a secure location? Any ideas?"

"It will take forty-eight hours to get all twenty-three members into one place. A couple of men are out of town and arrangements will have to be made," said Sean.

"Are you considering leading us?" Sid asked Jack.

"Yes, I am; however, I may require someone who will represent me here in Seattle. Any suggestions?"

"How about asking that question at the meeting," said Sean. "I'm positive the right man can be chosen if we put it to a vote. But, most importantly, we all have to vote that you'd be the man chosen to lead us," Sean said.

Sean told Jack the time and place of the meeting. Jack invited the three men to join him for dinner, but they declined. They left the restaurant at five-minute intervals.

Jack was elated! He was *in* and would soon be the mob's new leader. The only hurdle was the upcoming meeting, and he was positive that he would have little trouble in garnering their votes. He and his men returned to the hotel.

Jack Mostar was a careful man who seldom followed routine. Different routes were chosen to arrive at any destination. A second car always followed or preceded him. Sometimes he drove, other times he chose to ride on the passenger side or in the rear seat. He dressed similar to his three bodyguards to avoid being targeted by rivals. His dining habits seldom followed any routine, and he never repeated eating in any restaurant in the same week. Dining reservations were set at different hours each evening. One of his bodyguards, who prided himself with his cooking abilities, usually prepared breakfast and lunch, which minimized security issues.

To celebrate the success of the upcoming mob takeover, he made a ten o'clock reservation at a popular Italian restaurant, noted for its superb cuisine. When they arrived, they parked the cars in a corner of the restaurant parking lot and went inside. They were fifteen minutes early and tipped the headwaiter fifty dollars for their table of choice, this time, in a discreet corner table against a wall. They started by ordering drinks. All were in great spirits by the time dinner was brought to their table.

—

While they were inside the restaurant, Matt and Charles entered both vehicles to prepare the next phase in the capture of Jack Mostar. It took them forty minutes to complete their task.

—

Three hours later, Frank and his men left the restaurant. Only three vehicles were parked on the lot. One of the nearby vehicles was a black Chrysler van.

Once inside the cars, three events took place. The cars wouldn't start, the doors automatically locked and a hissing noise could be heard. Both cars started to fill with a fast acting sleeping gas. The occupants of both cars started to panic when they couldn't open the doors and started banging on the windows with their fists. Their panic served to make the gas work faster and thirty seconds later they started to pass out. Frank was the last to succumb.

Matt and Charles gave it an additional two minutes before they cautiously approached the vehicles and found the unconscious occupants. The doors were opened, the gas canisters were removed, and Jack Mostar was transferred to their van. Both cars were re locked, leaving Mostar's sleeping men inside, with their weapons. They would be out for at least twelve hours.

They loaded him into the secret compartment of the Learjet an hour later. The usual injections were administered, and he was fitted with the new hiking boots. Only one task remained. A detailed note, explaining why, where and when the mob members' meeting would take place, coupled with the location of Mostar's sleeping men; was sent by FedEx to the Seattle FBI. The Learjet left Seattle-Tacoma International an hour later, carrying the island's final prisoner.

Chapter 23

Judge Allen T. Petrick was awake and feeling lost, cold and confused. He was aware that he was underneath a blanket and was lying on cold ground. His neck, arms and legs ached badly. To start circulation, he started by rubbing his legs and discovered his wrists were bound! He was wearing boots and gloves! He managed to touch his face and discovered that something was very wrong. For years he had cultivated a beautifully coifed beard but discovered that it had been shaved off, leaving only stubble. Who had removed his facial hair, and why?

He was thirsty and could smell his own foul breath. Awareness started to permeate, and when he looked around, became aware of rock, trees and the sound of flowing water. He became alarmed when he saw the figure of a man sleeping beside him. It was too dark to make out the man's features, but it was evident that he was tall and slim and also covered by a blanket. The judge was afraid to move and continued to wait—though for God knows what!

Zachery Melcan was enjoying a dream about Evelyn and what she was doing to him. They were located in his bedroom, but the room was growing cold. Reluctantly, he started to wake up and discovered he had an erection! Then he discovered he was on cold ground, covered by a blanket and he too was wearing heavy boots and gloves.

He had never in his entire life awoken outdoors. He ached from head to toe, his tongue was as dry as sandpaper, and he was starving. His last recollection of food was the breakfast he had consumed at a roadside restaurant. He looked around and discovered forest and the sound of water.

He turned onto his side in order to relieve his aches and pains. Dawn was starting to give its' early light and Zachery found himself staring into the eyes of a man next to him. He was so startled, that he leapt up and discovered his bound wrists and an attached rope leading to a tree!

He looked at the man lying on the ground.

"What the *fuck* is going on? Where the hell are we?"

"My dear fellow," said Petrick, "I'm as confused as you are. I don't know how to react to all this."

Zachery looked around and discovered a number of stacked boxes. Stepping as close as the rope would allow, he discovered some bottled water and a windup flashlight. The first thing he did was to pick up a bottle of water, unscrewed the lid and completely drained its contents. He handed the stranger a bottle.

The judge gratefully accepted the water and proceeded to drink every drop of the precious fluid. Zachery grabbed the windup flashlight and awkwardly turned the handle a few times and managed to switch it on. A faint beam lit up the night and he pointed the flashlight around the area and discovered a note pinned to a tree. He almost stumbled over the judge in his haste to read the note. The judge arose and accompanied him, and they read the note together. They couldn't believe what they read.

Hello Assholes!

How does it feel to be on the receiving end for a change?
Read this carefully…

—

Jazz Hogue couldn't sleep and had been tossing and turning all night. He was growing tired of doing most of the cooking and chores, but was afraid to speak up. Bear and Chester were not the best of men and were, in fact, pretty scary. The only thing he enjoyed was cooking and splitting wood. He had progressed to making pretty good dinners—considering the crap he had to work with. For the first time in his life, he was getting himself into great shape by hauling water and splitting wood. He really didn't mind doing all the work, but resented the fact that everything he did was without appreciation on their part. They expected him to do it all! *Fuck it*, he thought, *I'm going to get dressed and go for a walk!*

He was beginning to enjoy his solitude when doing chores or going on lone walks around the island. He was about midway in his walk to the lower end of the island when he thought he heard voices. He became wary and moved from the path, trying to blend into the trees. He moved slowly towards the sound of the voices and saw a dim light in the distance.

He could see two men reading a note pinned to the large tree. He remembered reading the same note only three weeks before. He observed a tall elegant man in a suit wearing a fucking red bow tie of all things. The other man was shorter and pudgy and Jazz could see from where he was, that the man was shit scared! They went through the same antics as he had when he had first woken up on the island. He had to smile, as he observed their confusion. This was going to be fun! He decided to remain invisible and follow them to the cabin. He couldn't wait to see the look on the faces of Bear and Chester when they saw these two clowns. He also observed that there was only one pile of supplies and not two. He couldn't help wondering if their supplies HAD been cut as a result of the beating of Frank Herrick.

The tall guy must have rewound the flashlight because the intensity of light was increased. They passed him, clad in their blankets, and proceeded towards the cabin. Jazz followed, keeping out of sight and was almost jubilant as to what was to ensue.

—

The judge and Zachery stumbled and fumbled their way toward the cabin.

"Who do you think we'll find in the cabin?" the judge asked.

"How the hell do I know? Jesus, what a ridiculous fucking question!"

Zachery was starting to wonder who this prick was. He could also sense the fear in the man. Fear was starting to build in him too, but he sure as hell wasn't going to let it show—he was way above that kind of behavior! They proceeded in wary silence.

When the the two men arrived at the dark cabin a few minutes later, they were both freezing and, although they couldn't wait to enter, paused in trepidation—nervous as to what they would encounter inside. With a shaky hand Zachery opened the door.

"Is anyone home?"

"Who the *fuck's* there?" Bear bellowed.

"My name is Zachery, and there's a man accompanying me. We don't know where we are or who sent us, could you chaps let us in to warm ourselves? We are freezing!"

"Hold on while we turn on a fuckin' light!" Bear roared in reply.

There was a short pause while they cranked the lantern handle, and a light shone through the cabin window. They were told to enter slowly. Jazz followed them in and startled the two new men when he spoke.

"I followed them from the same spot where we all woke up. Looks like these are the new ones we expected."

Jazz closed the door and waited for the fun to start. It came quicker than he had anticipated. Bear took the lead, bellowing for effect.

"You in the cute bow tie, who are you, and why in the fuckin' name of Jesus are you here?"

"My name is Zachery Melcan, and I do not know why I was dropped in this weary destination."

"*Weary destination*—who the fuck talks like that? You sound like a fuckin' fairy dressed in that bow tie!"

The trio thought this to be quite hilarious, and they all laughed at the unfortunate new island captives. Bear leaped up to take a closer look at the terrified men. He told them not to move a muscle while he searched through their pockets. The only thing of interest found, was the red panties that Evelyn had tucked into Zachery's jacket pocket. Bear bellowed again.

"Are these your spare panties, or did you remove them from your fat friend here?"

Zachery turned a bright red and was speechless.

Chester spoke up at that point. "How about you model them for us after you two pussies warm up?"

Zachery was starting to get miffed. No one had ever spoke to him like this.

"You have no right talking to me in this manner, it won't do."

Chester slowly walked over to him and, while maintaining eye contact, sucker punched him in the stomach. Zachery went down like a stone. He found it hard to breath and was gasping for air.

"Hurts don't it, bitch? From now on," said Chester, "you'll do as we say, or there's more where that came from."

Jazz and Bear were surprised at the ferocity and swiftness of the attack. The judge had never experienced anything like this and decided to immediately change his identity. *From this minute on I am Timothy Nelson and I'm in the import business.* Zachery was slowly regaining his breath and was clueless as what to do next.

Bear quipped, "and who is your fat friend here?"

The Judge spoke hesitantly, "My name is Timothy Nelson. I'm an importer from New York and I do not know why I am here."

Bear was quick to speak. "You think you're here because you're innocent, you fat prick? You're here for some reason. You're guilty of doing something bad, or you wouldn't fuckin be here!

The Judge didn't bother to respond. There was no point.

They were left alone, while Jazz added wood to the stove and began to make food for the five. He chose to make a thick porridge and some rough homemade biscuits that he had recently learned to make from the sparse food supplies.

The smell of food soon filled the silent room. Bear was the first to help himself, followed by Chester and Jazz. The judge filled two bowls with porridge, added a biscuit to each and brought one over to Zachery, who was sitting, hunched over one of the bunks. He gratefully accepted the food and slowly began to eat. It wasn't half bad and at least sated their appetite.

Morning light started to sift through the cabin window and the lantern was switched off. The two new occupants were told to fetch water and bring in enough wood to fill the woodbin. They were told where to obtain coats from the storage area. They donned the heavy coats and hastily exited the cabin.

While they were gone, the trio exchanged a few words.

"So now there are five of us," said Bear. "I wonder if we can expect a sixth. I mean the note said there would be six, but I wonder if the last dead prick will be replaced? And are we going to get more food supplies I wonder?"

"There is only one stack of food out there by the tree," Jazz said. "I think the food supply has been cut in half as the note said would happen."

"What if they find out you punched the fairy? I think we better lay off with the punching until we find out the lay of the fuckin' land," said Bear.

"I'll lay off for now," said Chester, "but I sure don't like fairy pants! We have to find out why these two guys were sent here. Nothing makes any fucking sense!"

"I think I'd still like to see him wear those panties though!" And Bear laughed at his own funny comment. The other two laughed as well and this served to lighten the mood somewhat.

—

Outside, the two men walked down to the river to fill the empty bucket. They looked at the fierce river and the faraway land. The sky was starting to cloud over. It looked like a storm was on the way. On the return trip, the judge stooped to pick up firewood, dreading his return.

—

They reentered the cabin and were told to bring in the supplies from where they had arrived. As soon as they warmed themselves, they again left the cabin and trudged to the food supply. It took two trips, and by the time the last of it was carried inside the cabin, snow had started to fall. They were in for a snowstorm, and the wind was starting to howl.

Inside, all remained quiet. Jazz made coffee for everyone and retired to his upper bunk to read one of the cookbooks. Bear brooded, while standing at the cabin window, looking out at the fierce storm blowing in from the north. He was thinking of his past and knew that all he had built up in his life had probably disappeared by now. *My future ain't worth a pinch of shit unless I can get off this fuckin' island and soon.*

Chester lay on his bunk and also pondered his future. The mob would surely kill him because of his disappearance. His wife and child sure as hell wouldn't miss him. He thought of the beatings he had inflicted in his life. Bitter remorse for his violent past was settling in. What had he really accomplished? At least he had a lot of money hidden away in the Cayman Islands. *If and when I get off this fuckin island, I'll retire to somewhere safe—if there is such a place.*

Zachery was only thinking of Evelyn and getting Wartavan approved so he could repay his gambling debts and get back to work. He still had to locate and kill the Rawlins woman. And his present situation was awful. *Shit, I am even starting to miss talking to Mom and Dad. How the hell am I going to get out of here?*

Judge Allen T. Petrick was feeling sorry for himself. What had he done to deserve the company of people such as these? He missed his Scotch and his little pleasure room—and suddenly a thought occurred to him. Whoever had captured him must be aware of his little collection. He had to get back and get that situation under control, and soon, or his career as a judge would soon come an end.

—

Jeff was fascinated by what he was seeing. The way everything was unfolding was like something out of a novel. For whatever reason, he found himself disliking Jazz Hogue and wondered why. As far as the sucker punch administered to Zachery Melcan, he would let that one go for now. If any violence were repeated, however, he would cut the supplies again. He was starting to realize that the form of justice he was witnessing was starting to make up for his family's murder.

He missed them so much that sometimes he wanted to curl up and cry like a baby. He wondered how Matt was making out with the final inhabitant of the island and thought that Matt was due for a bit of a break. His schedule during the last three weeks had been brutal, and he'd looked tired the last time he'd been here.

Jeff's SAT phone rang at that moment, and Matt was asking for an update.

"As you can imagine, things started out tense, but they've cooled down a little now."

"Anything I can do?" Matt asked.

"Nothing that I can think of. I find it very interesting the way everything is starting to unfold. All six, including the now departed Frank Herrick, were at the peak of their power before they were whisked away. They're all completely stunned and don't know what to do. The other thing they have in common is that they're not sharing any information with each other, as to their true identities or divulge any of their pasts. They may all be thinking that the others are members of some police agency, trying to elicit information."

"Jack Mostar will certainly change the group dynamic," said Matt.

"How so?"

"I think he will somehow try to gain control of the group."

"That didn't work too well for Herrick," said Jeff.

"True enough. Well, too soon to say, but you can bet his being there will change things a fair bit. The guy is clever and will probably be the most dangerous."

"Looking forward to it. Matt, why don't you stay here for a few days after dropping off this Mostar character? I noticed you looking a bit tired on your last trip."

"I think I will. I think we ALL need a break!

See you soon," said Jeff, "and when you get here we'll celebrate."

"It's a deal."

And with that, they signed off.

Chapter 24

At his FBI Seattle office, Wes Harrison was both elated and dismayed.

The good news was the lead that he had received via FedEx this morning, pertaining to the mob meeting that was to take place later in the day. The second lead, from the same source, resulted in the capture of three gang members belonging to Jack Mostar. They had been rounded up earlier in the day and were still unconscious! The three had unregistered weapons on them, and two had cocaine in their possession. Wes couldn't wait for them to wake up. It was still not clear what had knocked them out. Four sets of fingerprints had been found, and three sets belonged to the trio. It was assumed that the last set belonged to Jack Mostar. He was still awaiting the match. The car had been reported stolen only a few days ago and he had the three men dead to rights on that score. All three gang members were known to them and were real bad Asses.

But the big question was the whereabouts of Jack Mostar. He had not checked out of his hotel and had yet to use his return air tickets to New York. The assumption had to be that whoever had subdued the gang members had abducted Mostar—but to what purpose?

FBI teams had been dispatched to the warehouse where the mob meeting was to take place. If his information was accurate, approximately twenty to twenty-five of Gino Danelli's mob would be present at the meeting. All gang members were wanted men, and up to this time, had been in hiding. The evening would prove interesting!

All this was great news, but the bad part were the files of missing people he currently had in front of him. All were influential individuals of questionable character. They included: Jazz Hogue, Harry Blankford, Frank Herrick, Chester Bennett and now, *Jack Mostar*. Zachery Melcan and Judge Allen T. Petrick were also questionable, but on a different scale. Melcan was the head of a pharmaceutical company and Judge Petrick was the New York judge who had let Mostar walk away from a murder wrap. There appeared to be a strong connection; and coincidence that Mostar AND the Judge had disappeared at about the same time. The other coincidence was Chester Bennett and Jack Mostar. The last four were definitely connected. Wes Harrison did not believe in coincidence. All had vanished without trace, and though none of the seven would be missed, all presented loose ends and required closure.

What was the connection? Why and how had they all disappeared without trace? The FBI and all law agencies combined had yet to come up with one solid lead! Something just wasn't right. Seven individuals were missing, all influential in their own right, and all missing. It was like some giant hand had reached down and scooped them out of existence.

Maybe the rounding up of Danelli's mob would turn up something. The ringing of his phone interrupted his thoughts. His team leader for tonight's raid was on the line.

"Everything is ready for tonight's operation. I'm thinking that we should listen in on their meeting before we scoop them up. Maybe we can learn a little about why so many men are disappearing?"

"I agree," said Harrison. "It certainly won't hurt to wait. Do we have enough men for our roundup?"

"We have forty people in place, plus the whole area will be cordoned off as soon as everyone is accounted for at the meeting. The net will be very tight. The meeting should break up pretty quick, unless Mostar shows up."

Wes signed off but assured the agent that he could be reached at this same number until the operation was complete. Tonight's raid was crucial, and he wanted no screw-ups. He reluctantly returned to the files regarding the missing men.

He began with Jazz Hogue. Jazz was a small-time dope dealer who had come up the hard way. He was a suspect in a few murders, but always managed, at the last instant, to sidestep any convictions. He had been on their watch list a long time. Wes was waiting for him to lead the FBI to bigger fish—that is until he pulled the vanishing act.

Harry "Bear" Blankford was another drug dealer who had also eluded arrest. His two associates, small-time hit men known collectively as C&C had dropped out of sight about the same time as Blankford. The only thing the FBI came up with on the two men was that both had lost a finger prior to disappearing. *What the hell was that all about?*

Then followed Frank Herrick, who disappeared the same time as his Paris Chateau, his LA mansion and his supposed drug lab, which had all been blown to hell. Herrick was a kingpin in the LA drug world and not one agency had even come close to nailing the son of a bitch. His five henchmen were now out of the picture and keeping low profiles. Herrick's office safe was found empty and his delivery service company had yielded nothing. Herrick and company had been wiped clean!

There was another coincidence; Chester Bennett had also vanished. He had been Dino Danelli's accountant and possibly connected to the disappearance of Danelli's bank accounts. Bennett's wife and son were missing too. Had the family run off together? By all reports, Bennett and his wife were not close, but that didn't mean much. Bennett just didn't seem to be the type to tread on the toes of a man like Danelli.

And what had been the purpose of Jack Mostar's visit from New York? Another fucking coincidence! It all pointed to the possibility that perhaps Mostar wanted to take over Danelli's operation. He had visited Dino's wife and spent a few hours with her. She sure as hell wasn't saying anything! Would Mostar show up at tonight's meeting?

Zachery Melcan couldn't possibly be connected to any of the above— *or could he?* Yet he had pulled a vanishing act around the same time. He reportedly had gambling debts at two casinos, but Wes doubted they would do away with him. After all, he did have enough collateral to pay them off. His pharmaceutical business seemed to be flourishing.

And last but not least there was the disappearance of a Federal Judge! Again, around the same time frame as the others! Was there a connection? Judge Allen T. Petrick had ruled in Mostar's favor in regard to his New York murder conviction. Jack Mostar and the Danelli mob profited from the ruling. Child pornography had been found in the federal judge's home—a lot of it! And finally, the unexplained five hundred thousand dollar deposit to the judge's bank account, shortly following his ruling. *Curiouser and curiouser!*

Had all these men been eliminated? And if so, by whom? Why was it being done? Was it motivated by revenge, or was it perhaps the muscle of a rival drug cartel?

Wes Harrison was beyond impatient—*still not a single fucking clue!*

Plus he was getting anxious about the evening mob roundup.

—

Sean was one of the last to enter the warehouse. All twenty-two gang members had arrived! He knew them all by name. He was hoping they would accept Jack Mostar. Furthermore, he was also hoping that he would be put in charge of the Seattle operation on Mostar's behalf. He had his sights on Dino Danelli's Villa—and his wife. He and Louisa Danelli had always been friends. He didn't mind the kids either.

Where the hell is Mostar? The bastard's probably waiting to make a grand entrance. Fuck it. Might as well get the ball rolling. He strode to the centre of the warehouse and found most of the men standing, while a few sat on crates. A single bulb, high above, provided a dim light. The men were growing impatient and tense and vulnerable. They did not like being all together in one place. All were seasoned criminals, and Sean knew they were responsible for many killings and all forms of violence. The one binding element was their loyalty, and right now they badly needed leadership.

Sean cleared his throat. "You all know that Dino and Bruno have been arrested by the FBI, and it doesn't look like they'll be back with us for some time. Right now, it's up to us to reorganize and keep things going. We need to vote for a new leader tonight, and I have just the man in mind."

Uneasy silence and the shuffling of feet greeted him. Butch Daruzzi, who was noted for his brutality and longstanding loyalty to the Danelli mob, cleared *his* throat.

"What do you fucking think will happen if Dino finds out about this new leader?"

Grunts of agreement were heard and Sean spoke again.

"I think you'll all agree with me that Dino will always be our leader, and if and when he returns, he'll assume leadership once more, and I'm sure you'll all back me on this. But right now we have to survive. It's like he's on vacation, and he's expecting us take some initiative and keep things going."

Butch again spoke.

"Do you think he's enjoying his fuckin' vacation?

The tension had finally broken and chuckles and laughter were heard throughout the group. *What was keeping Mostar for fuck sake! This was getting serious!* Sean had to come up with something fast or things would start coming apart.

"I know a lot of you have heard of Jack Mostar from the East Coast Division. He runs a tight ship, and his men have been with him from the beginning. I know Dino was happy the way he ran things. I'm proposing that he assumes temporary leadership, unless one of you has any better ideas. Mostar is proposing to control things from the east for now. He's asking that one of us runs things at this end. He is also suggesting that we continue to operate as we always have."

Sean held his breath while the men mulled this over.

"Why isn't he here," one of them asked, "if he's so interested in leading us?"

Sean answered that right away. "Because he wants us to decide on our own and has asked me to put it to a vote, unless you can come up with anyone else. It's up to you."

"I think," said Daruzzi, "that we should meet again in a week, but this time, Mostar should at the meeting. This'll give us time to talk it over and find out more about this guy."

All the members voiced their approval to Butch's suggestion.

Sean knew he would get no further, but knew he had made some progress. He was also thoroughly pissed with Mostar, who had put him in a very awkward position.

"I agree with you and I propose we meet here the same time next week."

The meeting broke up quickly, and everyone started to exit the warehouse. As they emerged, bright spotlights and car lights suddenly blazed and a voice spoke at them, using a loud haler.

"Hands above your heads. This is the FBI, and you're all under arrest! Don't even think about going for your guns or we'll open fire! Those of you inside are not to move, as we have men inside with orders to fire at anyone who moves! You are completely surrounded"

Butch Daruzzi was the only one who went for his gun, and he was immediately shot through both legs by sniper fire. The twenty-three gang members raised their arms and were quickly disarmed. They were handcuffed and loaded into FBI vehicles. Sean was the last to board and livid beyond belief. With all his experience, he had only posted two guards, reason being, he had wanted most men on the inside, in order to garner their votes. Who the fuck had set them up? He could only think of Jack Mostar! Now he knew why Mostar failed to show. *The bastard is a walking dead man. Sean also knew he was also in deep shit, as he was the one responsible for setting up this fiasco.*

Chapter 25

His goal had finally been reached, and he was king of the hill. Jack Mostar was a happy man! He was dining with a beautiful woman in his brand new Italian villa overlooking the Adriatic Sea. The setting sun was spectacular—but why was it so cold! Jack was starting to shiver; his dream rapidly began fading as reality set in. He was wearing a heavy coat and boots. He had mittens on his hands. A blanket was covering him and he could feel snow against his skin. His arm ached and he had a foul taste in his mouth. He was thirsty, hungry and confused. Night was being replaced by early dawn. *What the fuck is going on?*

He suddenly was jolted awake when he remembered passing out in the car. Jack had no clue where he was. It was early dawn, and only the sound of flowing of water could be heard. He remembered the upcoming meeting with all the mob members; it was a meeting he could *not* afford to miss! He leapt up and frantically looked around. He needed to determine the time, but found that his watch was missing and his wrists were bound together and attached to a rope leading to a nearby tree. He became aware of a stack of boxes with a flashlight perched on top. It was a windup light, and he cranked the handle a few times, flipped the switch and was rewarded with a beam of light. He pointed the flashlight in several directions and noticed a note pinned to the tree that he was tied to.

Hello Asshole!

How does it feel to be on the receiving end for a change?
Read this carefully, and you may live to see another day…

—

Most of the inhabitants of the cabin were sleeping. In one of the upper bunks, Zachery was waking to the new dawn. He was unshaven and dirty; he could smell his body odor. For a man who was in the habit of showering and shaving twice daily, he was disgusted with himself. The cabin stank of unwashed bodies and stale cooking odors. He was unsure, afraid and had felt that way ever since arriving on the island. The only thing keeping him sane, were the memories of Evelyn Twain. He reached into his pocket and fingered her panties. His thoughts again turned to their evening of rapture.

—

In a nearby lower bunk, Chester Bennett was thinking of his runs through the park, punching unsuspecting female joggers. Just thinking about it was starting to give him an erection. His thoughts shifted to how his father had dominated his mother. Chester had loved his father because of all they had done together. They fished, went to baseball games, movies and played hoops in the family driveway. He remembered the day that things changed forever. He and his dad had decided to take a weekend off to go on a real fishing trip! They were in great spirits as father and son packed the car and boat. The day was off to a glorious start. About two hours out, they stopped at a service station to have lunch and fill up with gas. They checked to ensure the boat and trailer were hooked up properly only to discover that they had left the boat's motor at home in the garage. His father was furious with himself and they had to return home to pick it up.

When they returned to their home, they discovered a strange car parked in the driveway. He and his dad went inside to investigate, and they found his mother in bed with a stranger. The man was able to grab his clothes, escape through a window, race to his car and lock himself inside.

His dad had run out of the house to try and catch him, but the man had managed to back the car up and, with tires squealing, made a clean getaway.

His dad really lost it at that point. He re-entered the house and confronted his wife. She defended herself by saying that she didn't like the way she was treated and didn't love him anymore. He knocked the wind out of her by hitting her in the stomach and then gave her a fierce uppercut to the chin, knocking her out. He kicked her several times for good measure and went into his office in the basement and started drinking. Chester had seen the whole thing and didn't know what to do. Their fishing weekend was ruined, and there would never be another one. His Father continued drinking and turned bitter. He would frequently punch his wife when she least expected it. Chester could still hear his voice.

"Hurts don't it, bitch?"

For some reason, she never left him and continued to take the physical and mental abuse that was handed to her. Chester was pretty much ignored from then on, and one day, at the age of fourteen, he simply packed a suitcase and left, never to return. He never forgave his mother for ruining their lives and vowed never to respect or love any female ever again.

—

Jazz was always the first to rise in the morning in order to add wood to the stove. The other men always left the morning chores including coffee and breakfast to him. Not that he minded, as it helped pass the time of day. The new occupants were a quiet pair and chose to share little about their lives. *We are all so fucking paranoid!*

—

Bear sat on the edge of his lower bunk scratching himself. What he wouldn't give to take even a short shower! He couldn't stand the two new assholes, and if it was up to him, he'd throw their sorry asses into the fuckin' river! The only thing holding him back was the threat of a cut in supplies. His rage over his captivity was growing each day. *He felt like beating the shit out of someone!*

—

Judge Petrick was feigning sleep and surveying his fellow prisoners through slit eyelids. He was dispirited, filled with fear and was definitely in the wrong place. *Or am I? Someone has judged me and sentenced me to this hellhole. A judge learning about punishment first hand!* He wondered if he was being punished for his addiction to child pornography or the crookedness during his years on the bench? He was surely atoning for his sins now and wished he could be given a second chance. He wished he could put things right again! *The future looked bleak indeed!*

A knock on the front door interrupted the silence, the latch was lifted and the door slowly opened. The sun was on the man's back, so the men could not make out his features.

"Am I late for breakfast?"

"Who the fuck is asking?" said Bear.

"My name is Jack Mostar"

Chester went pale and didn't say a word. Had the mob found him already?

Judge Allen T. Petrick certainly recognized him and went weak with fright. *How the devil did Mostar get here, and why?* The judge didn't believe in coincidence. The only time he had met him had been in his courtroom. As long as he stuck to his new name and the fact that his beard had been shaved off, leaving only rough stubble. He might not be recognizable. *I will have to play this very carefully! If this lot discovered that he was a Judge, he didn't even want to think of the consequences!*

"Well, welcome to our island paradise," Bear said disingenuously. "Will you be staying long? I do hope you brought your shaving kit."

"To answer your questions: no, I'll be leaving very soon, and sadly, I have no shaving kit, as I was caught somewhat unawares."

"So you plan on leaving our fine company quickly, eh?" Bear sounded humorless. "What time is your yacht picking you up?"

"Who wants to know?" Jack asked

"My name is Bear, the guy beside the stove is Jazz, and the guy standing beside his bunk is Chester. The other two are the latest arrivals—before you that is—the tall lazy fag sitting on the upper bunk is Zachery. The fat scared prick that's pretending to sleep, calls himself Timothy. One guy has already died and is buried by the river. Never did find out his name."

Jack seemed to be taking everything in at once. "How did you guys get here?"

"The only fuckin' thing I remember, before being brought here, is someone shooting me in the neck with something. The next thing I remember, I was waking up at the same spot where you probably woke up. The same dart thing happened to Jazz and Chester. Don't know about what happened to the last two. What about you?"

"My men and I were gassed in our car," said Jack. "And here I am."

"This is gettin' fuckin' creepy," said Bear. "How about you two fags? What happened to your sorry Asses?"

"I think I was darted too," Zachery said.

Petrick said, "I was drunk, and I woke up here."

"So, now we know *how*," said Jack. "And I guess the *why* is none of my business. Obviously, the same party is doing this to us. But enough of this for now, what's the chance of a cup of coffee and a bite to eat? Jack's voice was cheerful and nonchalant.

The tension was broken and the mood of the group relaxed a little. They were all fascinated by this latest arrival. Jazz poured six cups of coffee and handed one to Mostar. The rest came over, and each man selected a mug. They also helped themselves to the thick porridge cooking on the stove, along with a cold biscuit. They ate in silence and finished their coffee. Jazz left the group, to make a fresh pot.

Mostar asked to read the second set of instructions. Jazz handed it over. They sat in silence, until he finished reading.

"Makes for interesting reading. Whoever's put this little party together is clever and very well connected. We must be under their scrutiny. They're controlling things tighter than we think. I'm thinking we're somewhere north because of the cold and snow. The population must be sparse up here and isolated as well. We're hard to spot from the river and air. Whoever picked out this spot is pretty fucking clever. In order to get off this island, we have to get a lot smarter. Anybody interested in helping me bring over my supplies?"

So easy, he thought. *I already have these stupid bastards just about in the palm of my hand. I'll motivate them to help me escape and then leave them here to rot for all I care. How could they allow themselves to get so filthy? They look like bums. Time somebody whipped them into shape.*

The group's mood continued to lift. They needed proper organization, and this was the prick to lead them. Bear, Jazz and Chester volunteered to help with the supplies. They dressed for the cold and left the cabin, while Zachery and the judge stayed to clean up the cabin and do some of the outdoor chores. They talked as they worked.

"I wonder where this leaves us," said Zachery. "Should we trust this Mostar guy?

"I don't know what to make of him. Did you notice how fast he gained our confidence? He's a born leader, and I think he will protect us from the other two. I think he's clever but *very* dangerous. I also think he'll use us to accomplish his goal of leaving the island. I'm going to be very careful what I divulge to him."

Zachery was impressed with that assessment of the situation and wondered what Timothy had done to be sent here. He just didn't fit into this group. For that matter, neither did he.

"You make good points, and I think you're right, we'd be wise to watch what we say around this guy. *I think he's more than dangerous!*"

Chapter 26

The cabin's activity had been monitored ever since Jack Mostar's arrival, and Mostar had not followed in the doomed footsteps of Frank Herrick. He had carefully surveyed the island, the river and the cabin. Mostar had slowly walked to the cabin, knocked and entered. From that point, he started to control the men and completely changed its' dynamic. He was a natural leader, and it was obvious he was using the group to aid him in quitting the island. The method he would choose for his escape was not yet clear, but something was going to happen sooner rather than later.

The four men left the cabin to bring back the new supplies, and their conversation proved interesting. Jack Mostar asked what their daily routine consisted of and ingratiated him to them by asking how he could be of help.

"How about finding a way to get us off this fuckin' island?" said Bear.

"I already have something in mind, but I want to keep it under my hat until I've worked out some minor details."

"Can you at least give us a hint how you intend to bring this off?" Bear again asked.

"Please be patient with me, Bear. I've just arrived, and my mind is a bit overwhelmed with the situation. Also I'm a bit tired. When I have it fully figured out, I'll fill you in with the details, alright?"

"That's fair, as we've waited this long, and a day or two longer won't kill us."

"Can you tell me what happened to the dead guy?

Bear shrugged. "Sure, the prick came in and tried to intimidate us. We got pissed and beat him up. Then, one night he had a bad dream and woke us with his screaming. Chester and Jazz picked him up and threw him nearly naked out into the cold. I guess he caught pneumonia. The next day and he up and fuckin' died on us, the weak bastard! We buried him at the tip of the island and marked the spot with a rock."

Jack nodded. *What kind of idiot would show up and to try to intimidate Bear and Chester? A dead idiot, I suppose. Anyway, time to change the subject.*

"So have you folks tried to escape already?"

It was Jazz who spoke up this time. "Have you looked at that river? It's running cold, deep and fast. We tried making a raft, but it floated away during the night. I guess we didn't secure it well enough."

"Have you considered the possibility that our jailers untied the raft and pushed it off?"

"Nah. Don't think so. We couldn't find any tracks," said Jazz. "To tell you the truth, I wasn't too thrilled on trying the raft anyhow, because I really didn't think we could survive the river. We didn't build it all that well."

Silence ensued, and they picked up the supplies and returned to the cabin. It was growing cold and clouds were starting to gather. It felt like another storm was brewing.

—

Matt, Charles and Jeff decided to take turns listening in. Jeff would take the first four hours, as Matt and Charles were still fatigued from their recent trip.

It was now mid afternoon and Jeff kept himself alert. This Mostar guy was troubling him, and he found he was listening carefully to what would unfold.

—

Mostar asked if there was a knife-honing device available. Jazz handed him one from a drawer, and Jack began sharpening the jackknife that he had pulled from the tree.

The men carefully watched his efforts. He had Jazz heat some water, as he continued to hone the knife without explanation. When the water was hot enough, he poured some into a basin, stripped off all his clothes, grabbed a bar of soap and a washcloth and started to wash his body. He dumped the water outside and refilled the basin with more of the hot water. Then he lathered his face with the same bar of soap and carefully shaved, using the pocketknife. He managed to nick himself twice, but ten minutes later, he was cleanly shaven.

"Hey Jack, which restaurant you going to," asked Bear, clearly amused. "And does your date have a friend?"

Zachery brought over his jackknife and asked Mostar to give him pointers on how to sharpen it. When he was shown how, he repeated the same cleaning and shaving routine and was starting to feel much better. Jazz was next, for his chore was to prepare dinner. Jack promised him he would prepare the next day's dinner. The men followed his example, using the same body cleaning and shave routine. The mood was definitely picking up! Laughter and crude jokes could be heard during the meal. Jack had struck a very positive cord and for the first time since being at the island, tension finally took a holiday!

—

Jeff was amazed, and when Matt relieved him later, he was told the latest news. *I wonder what's next on Mostar's* agenda, Matt thought. *Things are definitely changing, but in what direction?* Jeff went off to join the others for dinner, leaving Matt to attend his shift.

—

Back at cabin, the six men were careful not to say too much about themselves and chose the safe ground by conversing about what they would do when they escaped the island.

"First thing I'm going to do," said Jazz, "is go to McDonald's and order myself two Big Macs, a double order of fries and a gallon of coke. Then I'll go home, put on a John Coltrane CD, and take a long hot shower!"

Bear said he'd buy himself the biggest steak in Seattle, while Chester said he would love to take a walk in a park and experience freedom once again. Zachery and the judge refrained comment. Jack was the last to speak before they all turned in.

"When we get out of here, I will throw you guys the best party any of you have ever had. Booze and girls, as much as you like of *either* until the sun comes up."

All went to bed and anticipated what the next day would bring. There was finally a glimmer of hope!

Jack Mostar had to content himself with blankets, as the current dead guy had been buried in his sleeping bag. He lay in his bunk and carefully planned the events of the next day. He had the thought that he wanted Bear to accompany him when he escaped. He also knew to be careful in voicing his plans, for he suspected that the group was being monitored. He was sure there was listening devices and wondered if there were any video cameras.

He was troubled by where he had seen this guy Timothy before. He looked vaguely familiar. And his voice: where had he heard that voice, and recently?? Then there was Chester Bennett. Somewhere in his past he had heard that name. And who and why was he brought here? But for now, he would concentrate only on escaping. He rolled over and fell into a troubled sleep.

Chester was curious as to how the escape would unfold and for the first time since getting here he was in a good frame of mind. He thought about a walk in the park and who his next female victim might be, once he escaped from the island.

Zachery and the Judge simply rolled over and blissfully slept. Chester and Jazz were already sleeping soundly.

The smell of scrambled eggs, bacon, biscuits and coffee was received very well the following morning. Jack did a credible job of cooking their breakfast. The ingredients he used were pieced together from the various freeze-dried supplies. When asked where he learned to cook, he answered that an aging aunt had taught him at an early age. He still enjoyed whipping up the occasional meal. The men couldn't wait for his dinner. Jack dressed, went to chop wood and fetch a pail of water from the river. All the men scrambled to do various chores and even swept the floor. Jazz boiled water and began washing his clothes for the first time since his arrival.

—

Meanwhile, Charles was observing all this with unbelieving eyes. What magic would Mostar next perform? Perhaps pull a rabbit from a hat for the evening stew? What would be the man's next feat? He was definitely establishing a leadership role.

Jack looked up to the cabin's peaked roof, just then, and seemed to look right into the hidden cameras. Charles swore that he was being winked at! This Mostar fellow was proving be a very shrewd fellow! Charles knew that the cameras were undetectable, but knew that Mostar suspected that they were being spied upon in some manner, and the high dark ceiling, seemed the most likely location!

Once the chores were done, Jack challenged them by asking who was game to do a morning run to the end of the island and back. All accepted the challenge with the exception of the judge. He only volunteered to take a brisk walk.

—

They're like schoolboys showing off to the girls! The sons of bitches are actually enjoying themselves! Charles yelled for everyone to join him and to witness this strange turn of events. Matt, Jeff and his two pilots rushed into the room, and were speechless with surprise. The runners ran and slipped their way from one end to the other. Even the judge was participating by following them at a brisk walk!

—

By the time they finished, everyone was breathless. They hadn't done anything like this since they were kids. What a mood they were in! They returned to the cabin and rested until they regained their breath. Jack suggested they go outside to have a private meeting. With lowered voices, Jack explained his plan.

—

For the first time, the observers couldn't hear a word being said.

—

Outside, Jack whispered that he and Bear would be the first to escape because Bear was the strongest and the power of the river was untested. When they reached the mainland, they would t steal a boat, return to the island and pickup the rest of them. *Of course, he had no intention of doing this, as they would only serve to slow him down. Speed was of the essence in getting back to Seattle to resume his takeover bid of the mob.*

Bear, of course, was all for the plan. Jazz and Chester were beginning to get a little uneasy. They looked up to Mostar's leadership, but he hadn't yet earned their trust. They would go along with the plan, but doubt was setting in. Zachery and the Judge didn't trust him at all, but were obligated to help in the escape plan. Just maybe, they would return to pick them up. *MAYBE!*

When the meeting broke up, they all started to perform various chores. Jack and Bear grabbed the two handed saw and started to cut a few logs. Jazz went to fetch water from the river and nonchalantly assemble the needed supplies for the escape. Zachery and the Judge carried firewood to the cabin and aided Jazz. Chester began splitting wood with the axe.

Late that afternoon, Jack Mostar performed the miracle of dinner. While a pot of water was boiling, cans of stewed meat and beans were opened, various packages of dried vegetables were mixed together and various seasonings were added. All was added to the boiling water. Flour was added as a thickener to the stew. He even made a batch of biscuits! Jazz carefully watched and learned some new cooking techniques. A fresh pot of coffee was made and good old Jack added salt to it, for added flavor!

Dinner was a raucous affair, and for the first time everyone was smiling and laughing. They turned in early, and the windup lamp was turned off.

All remained awake and were feigning sleep. An hour later, they all set to work, using darkness as a cover. They dressed and quietly went outside.

They dragged two of the precut eight-foot logs closer to the cabin. Mostar and Jazz then removed the hinge pins from the storage room door and carried it outside and placed the door onto the two logs. Zachery and Jack reentered the cabin and pried away the casings from the storeroom doorway opening, using the axe. They removed the nails from the boards and handed the nails and the axe to the waiting men outside. Using the axe, they pounded the nails through the boards into the logs.

Jazz carried the cabin lamp to the supply room, turned it to low lighting and assembled the food and miscellaneous items from a list Jack had handed him and rolled the contents into two sleeping bags. The sleeping bags were manufactured from a waterproof material and would keep the contents relatively dry.

Bear and Chester put on their winter wear, each attaching one of the now tightly rolled sleeping bags containing the supplies, to their backs, using a rough rope harnesses. All the men quietly left the cabin. Four of them lifted the makeshift raft and started carrying it to the opposite end of the island. Jack and Bear followed, carrying their supplies strapped to their backs.

All this activity was heard, but not seen by Matt and Jeff. Something was up! They heard hammering sounds. Also they heard scuffling noises from inside the cabin and the sounds of boards, being pried away from one of the doorframes and nails being removed. He suspected that some kind of raft was being assembled. They were planning to raft their way to land—and it appeared that they might just pull it off! Jeff asked Matt what could be done to prevent the escape. Matt was quiet for a few minutes before he replied.

"We'll let them escape and monitor their positioning by GPS, using our SAT phones. When they reach land, they'll travel until they tire, bed down and probably wait for dawn. Charles and I will organize an intercept and drive the ATV and trailer a half-mile from where they bed down. We'll sedate them and return them to the island. I intend to make sure these escapes won't reoccur! I'm sure Jack has promised them he'll somehow locate a boat and return for the rest of them. I'm also sure he doesn't intend to return. He's only using them to help with the escape."

GPS showed them that the six men were moving to the lower end of the island. After a short delay, two of the men suddenly separated from the four at a very fast rate. The remaining four made their way back to the cabin. The identification of the two departing men was Jack Mostar and Bear.

"How the devil are they going guide the raft to shore, I wonder," asked Charles. "The current in that river is treacherous! Look at the rate of speed they're travelling!"

"I don't know, but this Mostar hasn't missed a trick, so far!"

"What happens when we return them to the island?" asked Bob Cummings. "Will they repeat the same procedure, I wonder?"

"If they attempt it again, I have a couple of preventative measures in mind. Let's grab something to eat. I don't want to pursue these guys on an empty stomach. These two won't be easily taken down. I underestimated our friend Mostar. *I don't intend to underestimate him again!*"

Chapter 27

The four exhausted captives finally arrived at the cast-off point and happily lowered the raft to the shoreline of the river. Jack shook hands with the four remaining men, thanked them and told them that he and Bear would return, as soon as they found a boat. They were advised to have everything ready and for them to be prepared to leave at a moment's notice.

Jack and Bear dragged the raft to the river's edge, with Bear kneeling, facing the front of the makeshift raft, while Jack positioned himself behind him, also facing the front. Bear, being the stronger of the two, used one of the long handled shovels as an oar and had the job of keeping them away from rocks and keep the raft headed toward the shoreline. Jack would use the other spade as a brake and help Bear steer. They pushed off together and before they could wave farewell, the river grabbed the small raft and propelled them downriver at a frightening speed! They quickly disappeared into the darkness. The four watched the departure with alarm—they had not anticipated this much force from the river. Because they were growing cold and couldn't risk staying any longer, they quickly returned to the warmth of the cabin.

—

The force of the river both surprised and terrified the men, and they were feeling helpless. It had started out as a thrilling escape, but this was escalating into something out of a nightmare. The scraping of a rock against the frail raft galvanized them into action! The adrenaline kicked in, and they started to paddle for their lives. The river spun them around and they were now facing the wrong way and the two frantically worked together to try turning themselves around, but soon exhausted themselves in attempting to do so. Jack yelled to Bear to turn himself around, and Jack did the same. Jack was now in front and Bear was at his back. They shifted the shovels to their right hands and started to paddle to the closest shore but the opposite took place. The river propelled them to the far shore with such force, that they stopped rowing.

They had been carried approximately three miles from the island and at this rate, would double that distance before reaching the far shore. The raging river was driving them toward the rocky coastline at alarming speed. They were helpless, cold and getting wetter by the second. Now they could hear the sound of the river hitting rocks. Their tiny raft crashed into one of the rocks and started to tear apart. Bear's shovel was torn from his grasp and as the raft hit the rocks, he was catapulted into the air and crashed into a huge boulder with such momentum, that it split his skull. He was dead before his body slid back into the river and carried his limp dead body downstream.

Jack fell forward, slid from the raft, but managed to grab onto one of the rocks and hold on for dear life. When he finally managed to regain his breath, he was able to pull himself to the rocky shore inch by inch. He was drenched, cold and close to passing out.

He forced himself to stand and found, by some miracle, that his supplies were still tied to his back. He looked to see what had happened to Bear, but could only see a few feet, because of the moonless night. He found shelter in some nearby bushes and managed to find some dry driftwood. He unrolled the sleeping bag that had been tied to his back and found the matches that had been sealed tightly inside an empty foil food bag. Some pages, which he had ripped from one of the books in the cabin, were shoved into the same bag. He crumpled one of the sheets of paper and added it to the stack of driftwood and struck one of the matches against a rock. The end of the match broke off, as did the second. The third one lit and he fired up the crumpled page. Soon, the driftwood started to burn. He added more driftwood and soon had a warm fire going. *This fire, right then, represented the most precious thing to him in the world.*

The GPS indicated that Mostar moved a short distance and stopped. Bear, by this time, had begun to move at a slower speed downriver.

"What do you make of that?" Queried Jeff.

"I think they parted company with the raft somehow. Because their GPS positioning has come to a sudden stop and I surmise that the raft struck something close to shore. I suspect the raft broke up and Mostar managed to save himself." Commented Charles.

Matt brought up the GPS map coordinates on his computer and noted the location, confirming Charles's assessment. A half hour later, Bear's chip stopped suddenly, and ceased to move. His position was also noted.

—

Matt made the decision to visit both of these locations. It was decided that Jeff would accompany him and they hurriedly dressed and drove the ATV to the moored powerboat. It took them an hour to find Mostar's location. As they neared his position, they switched to the quiet running electric motor.

Mostar had gotten himself into a bad position. To his back, was a steep cliff, which rose a hundred feet, straight up. He was on a small, rocky outcrop; a pocket carved into the cliff, and would be unable to move either upstream or downstream. The river directly in front of him was swift, and the large jagged rocks would prevent any easy rescue.

They found themselves in a real dilemma. Should they rescue him, only to put themselves at risk and return him to the island, or should they leave him to his own resources. *He deserved the latter.*

—

Matt was satisfied that Mostar was now sleeping, so they turned their efforts to locate the whereabouts of Bear. The GPS showed them the way and thirty minutes later, they located his body. Bear was snagged onto an uprooted spruce tree, two miles down from Mostar's location. The boat was maneuvered close to the body and they managed to free it with some difficulty and wrestle his remains inside the boat. Bear's body was not a pretty sight. His skull was split, and a lot of blood had escaped through his skull. One of his eyes was hanging from its socket. Bruises and cuts covered his body. Jeff covered him with a blanket.

Matt did not feel any relief in the death of Bear, even though the man had killed his Father. He only felt a detached sadness. The man had finally met his fate. Bear was the second to die. Frank Herrick had been the first—the creator of the drug Crack'r Jack that had killed his son's friend. *The circle of life for the two men was complete.*

As dawn broke, Jack opened his weary eyes. He had had the foresight to include one of the sleeping bags, and although still damp, it had allowed him to remove his clothing and climb into it. The warmth of the fire had helped dry his clothes. At least there had been enough driftwood to keep the small fire going throughout the night. He was exhausted from the nightmare of a trip. He sat up to survey his surroundings and discovered that he was in an impossible situation. Escape from here was going to be virtually impossible. A cliff rose straight up behind him and the indent blocked him from going either left or right. The only exit was the river and there was no way he was going to attempt it a second time. Sharp rocks were sticking up everywhere. There was no sign of Bear. He had simply vanished. It was doubtful he could have survived the insanity of the river. The morning mist made the far shore invisible. He added more driftwood to the fire, turned over and went back to sleep.

By this time, it was an hour past dawn, and they headed the boat back towards the island. Their GPS pinpointed the location of the four inhabitants of the island. They were inside the cabin.

Twenty minutes later they beached their boat and quickly carried the body of Bear to the usual drop off point at the bottom of the island. A note was placed beside him with a rock holding it in place. They allowed the boat to drift away before restarting the electric motor, as they wanted to avoid any noise. They returned to the hunting lodge.

Chapter 28

Jazz was feeling a little pissed and more than a little confined. Pressure was starting to build since the departure of Jack and Bear, and for some fucking reason, he was missing their company a fair bit. Chester was just aching for a fight, and the other two creeps were keeping to themselves. On the plus side, at least they were being helpful with the chores. Chester was staring out the window. Zachery was whittling a piece of tree branch with his jack-knife and the fat Timothy was reading a travel book.

He decided to dress and go for a walk. None commented as he left. The fresh air felt good, and he needed the exercise. He sauntered to the island tip, glanced down at the grave of the man with no name and shivered. He looked longingly across the river to the shore. *God, I feel alone.* He walked to the lower end of the island using the now well-worn path. The weather was clear, cold and fresh. He was approaching the area where it at all began, when he noticed a figure covered with a blanket. A nearby note with a rock holding it in place was close by. With trepidation he cautiously approached and lifted the blanket. He screamed in terror at what he saw and ran as fast as he his legs would carry him, back to the cabin, with tears streaming from his face.

—

Chester was pouring himself a coffee, when Jazz banged open the door and began yelling hysterically. The startled Chester spilled coffee on his hand and cursed. Jazz continued yelling, Chester walked over to him, slapped him twice across the face, and demanded to know what the fuck was going on. Jazz managed to calm himself and explained what he had found.

"Bear is dead, his skull split open and one eye is hanging down over one cheek. He's covered with cuts and bruises!"

Zachery was the first to respond by suggesting they all go and investigate. The four men dressed and quickly proceeded to the spot. Chester removed the blanket and the three were revolted by what they saw. The judge went to a nearby tree and vomited. A shaken Zachery reached down and picked up a note held in place by a rock and read it to the group.

WELL ASSHOLES,

Your failure to abide by society's rules got you stranded here on this island. And now your failure to abide simple rules, have cost two of you your lives. Slow fucking learners.

We managed to find Bear snagged to a tree on the other side of the river. You were told not to go near the river! I suspect there was an accomplice and will keep looking for him. Rules are rules! Supplies have now been cut to one quarter. Try something like this again, and you can all starve to death for all I care! Society sure as hell won't miss you! When are you going to start cooperating and obey the fucking rules? Two people are now dead because of your stupidity!

The note stunned them, and not a word was spoken. They wrapped Bear tightly in the blanket and carried him to the same place where the first body was buried. They wondered how they would bury him. Both shovels were gone and burying him was going to present a problem. The judge came up with the solution. Why not simply place the body on the ground over the body that was already buried and cover him with rocks. A good supply of rocks and boulders littered the shoreline.

They all agreed and set to work carrying rocks to the gravesite and within two hours, the four men finished the task. The three shared similar thoughts. *Was this to be their fate too?* No prayers or final words were offered. What could they say? They knew they were bad men and didn't *stand a ghost of a chance* of getting off the island. A sense of doom descended on them as the trio silently returned to the cabin. Storm clouds were again starting to gather.

—

The observers witnessed the burial, and they too were quiet. Charles finally broke the silence.

"I suggest we concentrate on rescuing Jack Mostar and return him to the island. Leaving him where he is, will simply complicate matters."

Matt asked for suggestions as to how they should go about achieving this without endangering themselves. Bob Cummings made a suggested.

"How about lowering a rope ladder from the cliff, thus enabling the prisoner to simply climb out."

It was a good suggestion, but it would present the difficulty of being seen.

Dan O'Malley made an additional suggestion,

"How about throwing a rubber dinghy to him from the boat; then we could simply pull him over in the dingy and return him to the island. We will simply cover our heads with ski masks."

Charles came at them with a safer method of subduing Mostar.

"How about lowering drugged food to him from the top of the cliff while he's sleeping. Then when he eats it, we simply wait for the drug to take effect. One of us could row a dinghy from the powerboat and load him into it. We could then tow the dinghy to the island and drop him off at the usual place."

All agreed with Charles's suggestion.

They decided to wait until Mostar was asleep before making the food drop. It was also decided to wait for an extra day to ensure most of he food that Jack had brought with him was eaten—that way he would be ravenous.

—

Jack Mostar awoke at noon and feeling weak from hunger. He added wood to the still glowing embers and was soon warmed, and preceded to spread out his sparse supplies. Little was left. At best, if he stretched it, he had maybe a days supply. He opened a health bar and a small package of dried apricots. He drank from the river by cupping his hands. The water was ice cold. He surveyed his new prison. The size of the indent was about fifteen feet by eight feet, but at least the area was dry. The cliff rose straight up and canted out of sight. It was devoid of handholds and worn smooth as glass, by hundreds of years of wind and rain. He was in a bleak situation and was stumped at what to do next. He took off his boots and socks and ventured into the freezing water and tried for a peek around the rock cliff. The water was clear and deep and he could not see to the bottom. He tried the other side and found it worse. The current was impossibly swift and any attempt to try swimming around the abutment would be suicide. He quickly withdrew and returned to the fire to warm his feet.

At least there was an abundance of driftwood and fresh water. Jack froze, as he thought he heard the sound of a motorboat, but it was barely heard over the sound of the surging river and only lasted moments, then disappeared completely.

Is this how it ends? Clouds were gathering, and he knew that snow would soon follow. He gathered all the driftwood around him and placed it under a small indent in the cliff to keep it dry.

He stared at the river and was soon lost in thought. Boyhood memories flooded his brain.

He remembered the few friends he had had when he was eight and attending a slum school in West Bronx. Tim Warbrock assumed the role of his guardian. He was tough, rugged and was afraid of nothing. Jack was the opposite. Small of frame and spindly to boot, he recognized Tim's strength and weak mind and decided to exploit him to gain some protection. Jack would ensure that he always had an extra sandwich and stolen chocolate bars from a local grocery store. He knew that Tim was poor and always hungry, because of his size, so he began sharing his school lunch and fed him chocolate bars. From that point on Tim began looking out for him. Jack was now safe from the taunts of school bullies and gangs of young thugs.

He had learned a valuable lesson from that experience and soon learned how to exploit people.

Tim was killed, five years later, by a neighborhood gang. One young hood had snuck behind Tim and stabbed him in the neck, and *kept* stabbing him. He died in the middle of the street in a pool of blood. Jack knew that he would be their next victim, as he was now unprotected. He packed a bag and left home. His parents would not be missed, as they were seldom home and usually ignored him.

A gym owner, who befriended him, more or less adopted him; had him work out, using weights and punching bags. Jack progressed quickly and soon turned into a formidable fighter—was introduced to the right people. He learned about drugs early in life, and the first thing he learned was never to take any of them. At the age of seventeen, the mob took an interest in him because of his street smarts and fighting ability, and he quickly climbed the ladder of crime.

His thoughts returned to the present and he began to think that someone was punishing him for his past sins. But who the fuck was it? He had absolutely no idea who had gone to all the trouble and expense to bring him here.

—

The next evening, Matt, Charles and Jeff loaded the boat and re-entered the river. A storm was brewing and light snowflakes were falling and the wind was picking up. They again circumvented the island and Mostar's new prison. They beached the boat two miles downriver from him, and while Jeff stayed with the boat, Matt and Charles made their way to the cliff overlooking Mostar. It was near midnight, and they knew he would be asleep. They had to watch their footing, because the snow was making everything very treacherous. They reached the overhang and slowly lowered a burlap bag containing the drugged food. The bag was looped, using a double-length of small rope through an o-ring in the sack. It was lowered, and when they felt the bag come to rest on the ground below, simply released one end of the rope and pulled it through the ring and pulled up the rope. They headed back to the boat and returned to the hunting lodge.

Mostar woke up the next morning, covered in snow. While he was fetching firewood from his small stash, he spotted the bag containing food supplies. *How the fuck did that get here, and why didn't I hear anything? Jesus, this is creepy.* He found that he now had enough food for a couple days, but more importantly, someone knew he was here! There was even a thermos of coffee! He unscrewed the thermos lid and poured himself a cup of the precious brew. It was pretty good, although it left a slightly bitter taste in his mouth. He wolfed down one of the sandwiches containing lettuce, tomatoes and bacon. *It tasted glorious!*

He wondered what their next move would be. Somehow, they had to reveal themselves, which gave him hope of overcoming them and affecting another escape. The only way they could attempt a rescue was by boat, and he would be ready for them! He picked out a hefty piece of wood, which would serve as a club and inserted a couple of hefty rocks into the now empty burlap bag. He was ready for the bastards and sat down to wait. He wouldn't be caught sleeping again. *He found hope again, while he awaited their return.*

Chapter 29

By noon, their GPS indicated that Mostar had not moved. They were positive that he was out for the count and it was time for them to pick him up. A half hour later they approached his hideaway, using the boats' silent running electric motor, and beached upriver about fifty yards. Ski masks were pulled over their faces and they sprang into action. Matt climbed into the dinghy, which was secured to a nylon rope. Charles slowly played out the dinghy's rope, while Matt carefully steered the small rubber raft to avoid the many jagged rocks. The current was brutal and took longer than expected to properly position the small rubber dinghy. Matt felt like he was on a bucking bronco. He finally got close enough and to his relief finally entered into a calmer part of the river. He carefully entered the water and had the foresight to dress in a wetsuit, to avoid the freezing water. Once outside the dinghy, it started to bounce once more and Matt had to grab it with one arm, while attempting to swim with the other. He reached the shoreline rock shelf. This was going to be much more difficult than he had anticipated.

First things first. Get to Mostar. He lifted himself up onto the narrow jutting shelf, while still holding the bucking raft. He somehow had to drag Mostar to the bouncing rubber dinghy and lift him into it. The raft was pulled onto the lip of the narrow rock ledge. He approached the sleeping Mostar and carefully shook him. He was out like a light. Matt reached down, lifted the man to his feet and together, they entered the water. It took fifteen minutes to heave Mostar half way into the dinghy, and with a mighty effort he managed to heave the rest of him inside.

The rope that was tied to the powerboat had been rubbing against the cliff edge and was badly fraying. At the moment Matt heaved Mostar fully into the raft, the rope broke and the dinghy took off downriver, leaving Matt stranded. Matt yelled to Jeff to go after the disappearing dinghy and to pick him up later. They gunned the boat and roared after the now departing dinghy.

Matt was frustrated with his failure. He added driftwood and restarted the fire and hunkered down to wait for their return. Adding to their woes, dark threatening clouds were approaching. Within an hour heavy snow started to fall, and Matt couldn't see more than a few feet. He could imagine how difficult a time Charles and Jeff were having. He had put them in a very untenable situation and blamed himself for this unforeseen event.

—

Jeff and Charles were indeed having a difficult time. Traveling blind on this river was extremely dangerous. After an hour, they had little choice but to abandon the search for Mostar, at least for the time being. They had a difficult decision to make. First in abandoning the search and secondly, had little choice but to leave Matt where he was and make the dangerous journey back to the hunting lodge and regroup. They turned the boat around and headed back. Driving in this kind of weather required slow travel and a few times almost stalled the motor. As a result they had to increase their speed, which was also dangerous. Even at increased power the going was slow. To lose power on this river in these conditions was suicide. Added to this, more snow was falling and wind was blowing against them.

At one point, a rock scraped the boat and they realized they were too close to shore. They altered their course and ventured toward the center of the river. They were now relying solely on their compass, as they were starting to lose their sense of direction. Charles took out his SAT and dialed the lodge. Dan answered and was told exactly what they were facing. The phone was becoming erratic due to the changing weather conditions; but they were able to convey their idea. The two pilots would drive the ATV to the river and start honking the horn, as they were hoping the sound of the horn would guide them to safety.

Tension was building in Jeff's shoulders as he drove, and their situation was not improving. They kept fighting the river and the impossible conditions. The weather was worsening and the temperature was starting to plummet. One of the motors spluttered momentarily, causing their anxiety to worsen. Thirty minutes had now passed and the only thing they knew for sure was that they were going in the right direction. They badly needed guidance and soon, as the visibility was down to only a few feet.

They were wet from the snow and water was starting to slosh in the floor of the boat. The added weight made the motors run sluggishly, which resulted in increased fuel consumption. Jeff and Charles looked at one another with concern. Charles tried to reassure Jeff by patting him on the shoulder. *Despair was setting in.*

Chapter 30

Things were not going well for the inhabitants of the island either. Snow and wind was keeping the four captives cabin-bound and they were afraid to venture outside. Cold was setting in and wood had to be constantly added to the fire. The cabin's wood supply was critical, but neither of them wanted to venture out to replenish it. Chester added the final pieces to the fire and ordered Zachery and the judge to get dressed and yelled:

"Go get some more fucking wood!"

They reluctantly dressed and as they were heading for the door, Chester stopped them with his voice and amiably asked Zachery, if, once he returned to the cabin, if he would mind stripping, and putting on the red panties, adding:

"And the fat fag will be your bitch!"

They exited the cabin without comment and could overhear him laughing inside.

"I'm losing my patience with that prick," Zachery said, "and if he keeps it up, before long he is going to regret it."

"I wouldn't be too eager if I were you," Petrick said. "That man is a psychopath and not to be taken lightly. I have a feeling that anything you started would need to be an all or nothing proposition."

As they were bending down to pick up wood, Zachery thought he heard the faint sound of a honking horn, and wondered if he was losing his mind. The wind picked up and nothing further was heard.

"Did you hear that, Timothy?" Sounded like a car horn to me."

" It's probably the sound of Chester blowing his temper out his ass."

Both men laughed at that.

Without being seen, the judge hid the axe inside his heavy coat. He could sense that things were coming to a head and needed a little reassurance. With arms laden with wood, they returned to the cabin. Both hoped that Chester's mood would change for the better.

This proved not to be the case, however.

"What took you pricks so long?" Chester yelled as soon as they entered. "Were you two rehearsing your act for us?"

Jazz wasn't even going to attempt to comment, as he knew things were starting to get ugly. Chester repeated his earlier request and ordered both men to disrobe and for Zachery to put on the red panties and give them a show. By now, they both had taken off their coats and gloves, and Zachery finally lost his patience and told Chester to go fuck himself.

Chester slowly got up, walked over to him, and without warning, hit him viciously in the stomach. Zachery doubled over in pain and desperately tried to regain his breath. The pain in his stomach was intense and the punch completely emptied air from his lungs. He was finding it difficult to breathe and he came close to passing out.

"Hurts don't it, asshole?" said Chester and kicked him in the side for good measure.

This was the second time that Chester had sucker punched him, and it took Zachery a number of minutes to recover. He was in a rage! And Chester still wasn't finished with him and started yelling at him once more.

"I told you both to take off your fucking clothes, and I *meant* it!"

No one noticed, as Zachery reached into his pocket and pulled out his knife. He unfolded the blade and waited for the scum to approach him once more—he didn't have long to wait. Chester again strode over to administer another kick. Zachery rolled over and buried the razor sharp blade deeply into Chester's leg. The man went down hard and blood began poring from the wound as soon as Zachery withdrew the blade. Blood started to spurt onto the cabin floor. The blade had severed the main artery in his leg.

Zachery bent over and loudly shouted into Chester's ear.

"Hurts don't it, asshole!"

Jazz grabbed a soiled towel and held it to the wound to stop the bleeding. It soaked through the towel in seconds. He quickly removed his belt and looped it around Chester's upper thigh, using it as a tourniquet and pulled it tight. The flow subsided somewhat and the judge handed him a fresh towel to staunch the flow of blood once again. The floor was slippery with blood. Chester passed out and Zachery withdrew to his bunk. He still held the dripping knife and was awaiting further attack. None would come that night or any other. He was now a man to be feared and would never be touched by these or any scum like Chester for as long as he lived!

It proved to be a long night. Chester remained unconscious and in shock. The sound of his shallow, painful breath whistled out of his lungs. His leg was starting to turn blue and when Jazz loosened the belt, the blood continued to pour out of the wound. It was tightened again but failed to stop the flow. Chester was dying, and, the trio of men knew he had brought it on himself. What goes around comes around. These men weren't strangers to violence and death. And death was again making another visit to the island. Chester died in the cabin during the early morning hours, while a blizzard raged in the cold outside world. *A third burial would take place as soon as the storm passed.*

Chapter 31

Matt had never known snow like this. He knew rain and cold weather, but snow always presented hazardous navigating, regardless of what kind of transportation was used. This storm was huge and had blown in so fast, that he had failed to anticipate it. First there was the damn river and now the damnable cold and snow. He felt helpless and uneasy because of the conditions that Charles and Jeff were undoubtedly experiencing. He also was having difficulty dealing with his own situation.

However, he had been raised and trained to handle adversity, and handle it, he would! He retreated from the snow, by climbing inside Jack Mostar's sleeping bag and began thinking hard and long about what had brought him to this point in his life.

—

Meanwhile, the dinghy carrying Jack Mostar had just run into a reverse eddy near the opposite shoreline, propelling the small rubber craft onto the gravel shoreline and flipping him through the air onto a mound of hard gravel. His face was cut and bruised as a result, and one of his arms was twisted oddly, beneath him. He slept through it all and wouldn't be waking for several more hours because of the drugs still in his system from the drugged coffee. He emitted a painful groan and continued sleeping. The dinghy slapped back into the river and continued its downward journey. The heavy snow quickly covered him and, in an odd way, probably saved his life. It would continue to snow for several more hours.

—

For the first time in his life, Jeff was losing hope. He was tired beyond belief, getting colder and wetter with each passing minute, and the ache in his shoulders from steering the boat was unbelievable. Water level from the melting snow was adding to their woes. Charles was growing tired from bailing water with a small pail and was having difficulty keeping up. The weight of the water inside the boat was slowing them down and one of the motors was starting to cough. God knows what would happen if they stopped working. They had already witnessed the river's power and knew all too well the danger they were facing. The only thing they knew for sure was that they were still moving forward. They were in a white out. *The snow was not letting up at all!*

Another thirty minutes crawled by when they heard the sound of a horn, but it sounded like it was coming from *behind* them! They had passed the waiting ATV! Now to top it all off, they would have to turn around and that course of action was filled with danger. The decision was made to throw the boat into neutral and drift backwards. By doing so, this would cause the river to rapidly push them into a reverse position. The sound of the ATV horn was growing stronger now, and hope was building. Jeff shifted from neutral to forward and pushed the start button. After a few moments hesitation, only one motor restarted, but it was enough to slow the backward motion.

They started to inch forward once again and Jeff decided that the time had finally come and turned toward the still invisible shore. Snow was blowing directly at them, and for all intents and purposes, the snow was blinding them. A small crunch was heard and they thought that they had hit a rock—but this could not have been further from the truth. The boat had climbed up a slight embankment. The ATV horn sounded again, now very close.

"Hey, we're here, and we're safe!" Charles was shouting into the wind and snow.

"Take that, you fucking river, we made it!"

The two pilots walked towards the voices of their comrades and broke into smiles and shouts. They pulled the boat out of the water and onto dry land. Relieved hellos filled the air. They were driven back to the fishing lodge, a huge pot of coffee was prepared, and food was hastily made. An hour later, the pilots hooked up the trailer and went to fetch the boat. Dan O'Malley knew all about motors and his job was to check them and ready them for the next morning. He immediately set to work while the remaining trio held a council of war in the monitoring room.

Their first challenge was to rescue Matt, as soon as the storm ended and the motors were checked over and repaired. Supplies were readied and the cabin monitors were once again turned on. What they viewed, only added to their problems. They clearly heard the voices in the cabin as to what had transpired by using the playback. They managed to piece together what had happened. Chester had died from a knife wound to his leg and he would be buried, once the storm passed them by. *Three* captives had now died, one was missing and three remained alive! Plus, Matt was held prisoner in an impossible place. A course of action was quickly and carefully made. The only thing they could do now was to sleep and regain their strength to meet the next dilemma.

Dan worked until dawn. Both motors were fully repaired and tested. He stumbled off to bed, just before sunrise. It was a crisp cloudless day. The storm had finally run its' course.

—

Jack had never been in such agony. His body was covered in bruises and cuts, and he found that he could not move his arm. It felt like it was broken. *What the fuck happened?* He also found himself in some sort of snow cave. He was covered in deep snow and the only thing that had saved him from freezing to death was his own breath that had melted some of the surrounding snow. He was cold and wet. He painfully stood up, while cradling his broken arm with his good one and when he broke through the snow, he stood and surveyed his surroundings.. The snow had finally stopped, and the sky was clear. He found himself in a completely new place. *Where the fuck am I, and how did he get here? God, I am starting to lose my mind?* At least he was on the mainland now. He turned his back on the river and started to make his way towards a nearby tree line, slipping and sliding all the way, pushing through drifts as he went. After entering the trees, he walked about a hundred feet and found himself within a small clearing. To his right was a small, ancient cabin, which appeared to be abandoned. Standing between him and the cabin was a large lone wolf and it was staring at him!

He and the wolf had startled one another and both stood stock-still and simply looked at each other and after a minute, the wolf broke eye contact, retreated and disappeared into the trees. Jack walked cautiously to the cabin and knocked on the door. The cabin was silent. He unlatched the door and cautiously looked inside the small cabin. It contained only a small cot, a wooden rickety table, a broken chair and a tiny wood stove. To Jack, it was like heaven. On the table was a metal plate, a chipped mug, a knife and a fork. On the plate was a box of matches. Jack prayed they were still intact. He opened the box and discovered six of them. He found an old magazine by the stove, ripped out a few pages, crumpled them up and stuck them inside the old stove. In one corner was a neat stack of wood and a small amount of kindling, and leaning against the wood was an axe. He added some of the kindling to the stove, struck one of the matches and it lit on the first try. Soon he had a fire going and waited for the cabin to warm up.

He knew his most immediate priority was to attempt to repair his broken arm. He removed the belt from around his waist, made a loop and slipped his wrist into it. One of the eyelets of the belt was attached to a nail, protruding from a wooded beam. Now came the most difficult part. *Time to separate the men from the boys.* He would have to back up and stretch the arm full out, in an attempt to reset the bone. He did so until the belt tightened and stretched tight.

For some reason, his mind picked that instant to think of the toughness of his friend Tim, who had died years before—*what would ol' Tim have done in a situation like this one?* The memory of his tough friend made him stronger, and after three more painful tries, he thought that he might have finally manipulated the bones back together. He slowly released the tension, and although the pain came at him in waves, it felt that the pain was diminishing a little. He used a dirty towel that had been left behind and wound it as best he could around the break and removed the belt from his wrist. He removed the other end from the nail and looped the belt around his neck to form a sling for the arm. He slowly threaded his arm through the makeshift sling. By now he was so weak and sweaty from his efforts that he had to sit on the edge of the cot to rest.

The cabin warmed and his clothes slowly began to dry. He eventually had to stand again and added more wood to the fire. He returned to the cot, and, for the first time in his life, cried like a baby. His arm felt like it was on fire—the pain was unbearable. He lowered himself onto the old dusty mattress and fell into a painful, fitful sleep.

Chapter 32

Sitting on a large rock at the tip of the island, Jazz Hogue was enjoying the sunshine. Today was the warmest day he'd experienced since arriving here. *The snow is actually fucking melting!* He was glad to be away from the two fags in the cabin. He still couldn't figure out why they were here. They just didn't fit. He did give credit to Zachery though; he had had balls, stabbing Chester like he did!

At sunrise, the trio had carried Chester's body, wrapped inside a blanket, to the front end of the island and placed Chester on the ground, beside Bears rock-covered remains. It took them two hours to cover him with rock. As in Herrick's case, no words were spoken after the burial. While Zachery and the Judge walked back up the slope to the cabin, Jazz stayed behind to think.

Three people were now dead, all within three weeks. This was affecting him to such an extent, that he was reaching a breaking point.

At that moment, a speck of something coming down the river caught his attention. As it grew larger and larger, he realized what he was seeing! A huge uprooted spruce was floating toward him and the root end was going to soon hit the tip of the island. It didn't take Jazz long to figure out that when it struck, the tree would be pushed left or right of the island, by the power of the mighty river. He leapt back just before it struck the rock he had been sitting on. He made the fastest decision of his life. He grabbed onto one of the huge roots and climbed onto the tree and held on to a large branch and waited for the behemoth to dislodge itself.

A minute later, it started to fall away from the island. This was going to be the ride of his life. The tree swung around, and soon swept by the island. He yelled with happiness at the thought of escape.

—

When the two men in the cabin heard the yelling, they quickly came out to see what was happening. They couldn't believe it! There was Jazz, perched in the branches of the huge tree. It was quickly being swept out of sight, and as the tree gained momentum, they could hear his insane laughter—until both the tree and Jazz disappeared from sight.

They looked at each other disbelievingly and couldn't think of a word to say. It had all taken place so quickly. They both realized at that moment, that they might never see Jazz again. *Well, good fucking riddance!* Both disliked the man and had never fully trusted him.

—

Minutes later, Matt saw the approaching tree and saw a man perched onto it, clutching the branches for dear life. He swore he heard the man laughing insanely. The man and the tree came close enough to identify him. It was Jazz Hogue, and he had found a way to escape! *Shit, this is getting crazy. Somewhere downriver, on a dingy, was Jack Mostar.* All the careful planning was starting to unravel, and Matt couldn't do a thing about it. He wasn't even sure if Charles and Jeff had survived their trip back to the hunting lodge. He hadn't felt this helpless since the death of his father and wasn't even sure if he would survive, for there was no way out of his newfound prison.

—

The tree continued barreling downriver and hit the same place as the dinghy had struck the evening before. The reverse eddy and the swiftness of the river caused the tree to hit the shore so violently, that it made a large furrow in the bank, and before Jazz could jump off, the tree swung around and dislodged itself from the gravel embankment. All this movement caused the tree to turn over. Jazz started to scramble and *almost* made it to safety: until one of the branches snagged his shirt and carried him under the river's surface. In his struggle to free himself from his underwater prison, he panicked and inhaled water into his lungs. He started to choke and vainly tried to escape, but it was to no avail. The last thing he thought he heard before he died was the faint sound of John Coltrane on sax, playing a tune he couldn't remember—then everything faded to black. The tree continued its perilous journey downstream, carrying the river's latest victim with it.

—

Two sounds caused Jack Mostar to awaken. One was a distant crashing and the other was the howling of wolves outside his door. His arm was better, but not by much. He had to struggle just to sit up, plant his feet on the floor and push himself to a standing position. He walked to the cabin's only window. He looked outside—and froze. Jack had always thought that wolves only came out at night. These guys were huge, gaunt, mean looking and he could plainly see that he could very well become their next meal! He got the uneasy feeling that they had been gathering, ever since the lone wolf first spotted him earlier in the day.

Jack needed water. He was parched, almost to the point of dehydration. His only plan at the moment was to grab the plate on the table and, if he was quick, he could open the door and scoop up some snow before the wolves would react. He surveyed his latest adversaries and saw the closest ones lying in wait, while the rest were prowling a short distance away. He placed the plate in his teeth and using his good arm, slowly opened the door. All the wolves' heads turned toward him in unison. All were silent.

Jack slowly removed the plate from between his teeth and scooped a plate of the precious snow. Just as he closed the door, a large wolf, coming around from behind the cabin, launched himself at the door. Jack put his back to the door and in so doing, dropped the plate of snow. The wolves, as one, came closer and began to howl and snarl at their prisoner. It felt as if they knew he had a broken arm and were closing in for the kill.

Jack raced over to the table and with his good arm, dragged it to the door. He stooped to pick up as much of the spilled snow as could, and then simply sat on the table, which was the only defense; against the crazed wolves. While seated, he drank in the small amount of snow. It wasn't enough, but it would have to do, for he dared not open the door a second time. The wolves began launching themselves at the cabin door.

—

It was indeed a glorious day, and the sun was starting to warm up the frozen earth. Matt decided he had to do something while he waited for rescue. At least he hoped he would be rescued—he was still worried and still feeling terribly guilty for the precarious position that he had placed on Charles and Jeff. *I hope to hell they made it back ok!*

To relieve his tension, he decided to do some exercise. He started by running on the spot; this was followed by fifty push-ups and deep knee bends. He was in the midst of doing some jumping jacks when he heard the faint sound of a motor. The sound slowly intensified, and he soon spotted his rescuers! With relief, he waved and started to shout his hellos.

Charles and Jeff shouted to Matt,

"The only safe course of action for us, is to proceed down river and make way to your position from above and lower a rope. You can then simply pull yourself out."

They drove the boat about a mile downstream, beached it in a safe place and slowly made the difficult precarious climb. The going was treacherous because of the deep snow and slippery conditions. It took them longer than expected to reach the point above Matt.

They lowered a rope, and Matt grabbed hold of it and started to climb out of his prison. He was familiar with this type of ascent from the years he had spent in the military, but it was still a long difficult climb—it took him ten minutes to arrive at the top.

He was fed sandwiches and hot coffee once he regained his breath. They were all relieved to come together once again. Their first plan was to return to the lodge and view the monitor before tracking down Jack Mostar. When they reached the boat thirty minutes later they heard the sound of howling in the distance. Daytime howling was unusual in the wolf world.

It had been a tough twenty-four hours and the tension was greatly relieved when the five men reunited back at the lodge. They proceeded directly to the monitoring room, to determine the whereabouts of Hogue and Mostar. The GPS tracking devices were activated and it was noted that Jazz was miles downward, but still on the river. The GPS was used to pinpoint his location. It didn't look good. No movement was detected from Hogue's tracking device.

The GPS next picked up a signal from Mostar's position. He was ashore and movement was detected. Charles decided to try a direct feed by satellite, and by a miracle, it was in perfect position. Jack Mostar appeared to be in a cabin and shapes could be seen running around it. They realized that those shapes were that of the wolves they had heard earlier.

Matt, Charles and Jeff grabbed rifles and ammunition jumped into the ATV, and raced to the boat!

Chapter 33

Wolves were hurling themselves at the small cabin door. He knew that if he stood up and removed himself from the table, the wolves could easily break through the flimsy door. He waited for a lull to their charges and quickly ran to get the axe and ran back to lean against the table. At least he had a weapon to defend himself, even though he was one-handed. Holding an axe in one hand was hardly a defense, but he had never backed down from a fight in his life, and wasn't going to start now. His broken arm was on fire; he was weak from hunger and so very thirsty.

In his delirious mind, he remembered the last time he had a cold beer. It was at an outdoor restaurant during a long hot spell in New York. He and his men had had a great time that day and it was one of the few times in his life that he had gotten drunk. Deep down, Jack Mostar knew that he would never again have another beer!

Two of the wolves hit the door at the same time, breaking the spindly door catch. Now the only thing holding them back was the table against the door and Jack leaning against it. The wolves seemed to sense his helplessness, and the snarling pack was relentless in their attempt to get inside. One of the larger beasts leapt up and crashed through the window, but luckily he got hung up on the windowsill. Jack swung his axe the best he could with one hand and succeeded in splitting open the huge head.

The pack went wild and started to tear the huge animal to shreds and dragged it from the window. The dominant female ate her fill before letting the rest of the pack consume the remains. Jack was starting to weaken. The effort to keep the wolves at bay caused the re-breaking of his arm and he was starting to grow dizzy from the searing pain. At least the wolves were temporarily distracted and the lull allowed him to prepare for the next onslaught. He hoped the appetite of the pack would be sated enough to discourage them from trying again. What to do now? He walked painfully to the chair and broke away one of the legs. Now at least he had a small club in his arsenal. Jack once again put the metal plate between his teeth, pulled the table away from the door and opened it. This time the wolves were distracted enough so that he was able to scoop up a full plate of snow and reclosed the door. He picked up the table knife and wedged it between the door and the doorframe. The table was once more pushed against the door and he sat on the table again and consumed the plate of snow. He felt a little better, but he knew things might get a lot worse.

He waited for the next attack.

—

Time was of the essence, and they could not afford to spend time searching aimlessly. Their GPS guided them to Jack Mostar's position. The trio in the boat had the feeling the day was not going to end well. The rifles were loaded and readied. It took them thirty minutes to reach the proper river embankment. They beached the boat, grabbed the rifles and ran towards the cabin, hoping, they would reach Jack Mostar in time!

—

This time, two of the wolves entered the cabin by jumping through the window, while the remainder of the pack took turns launching themselves at the door. The door held, but now Jack had to deal with two of the vicious, slathering wolves. One of them leapt through the air, aiming for his throat, but Jack, now operating on sheer adrenaline, managed to bury the axe into the animal's neck—its momentum continued, however, and knocked Jack to the floor and landed on his broken arm. He heard several shots and heard yelps of pain from dying wolves. The remaining wolf inside the cabin chose that moment to go in for the kill! Jack was utterly helpless now, and the only thing he could think to do was to try to hold the animal at bay by glaring at him. It was not to be.

The wolf went for Jack's throat!

—

Matt shot two of the wolves while Jeff and Charles managed to shoot two others. The remaining five wolves ran off, and all suddenly grew quiet --- except for faint growling sounds inside the cabin. Matt ran to the cabin door and when he kicked it open, saw the horror within. He took quick aim and fired twice into the remaining wolf. Matt looked into the eyes of the dying Jack Mostar. Jack locked eyes with his rescuer, smiled painfully, and went still. Blood was pouring from his neck, forming a red pool around him. Warm sunlight shined into his lifeless eyes.

They saw that Jack had fought fiercely, despite his broken arm and had succeeded in killing two of the largest of the wolves. He *was a fighter* to the end. They observed that three of the dead wolves were rabid, which was probably the reason for the ferocity of their attack.

Jeff silently returned to the boat to fetch blankets and when he returned, they wrapped them around Mostar's body and carried him back to the boat. His body was gently lowered into the bottom of the boat. Few words were spoken as they departed.

Jazz Hogue's body was discovered thirty minutes later, still tangled in the branches of the huge tree, which had finally beached itself on a rocky shore.

They maneuvered the boat close to the tree. They had to use knives to cut him free. Jazz Hogue was not a pretty sight. Bones were broken, much skin had been ripped away and his frail body had been cut to ribbons. They laid him beside the body of Jack Mostar and covered him with the last of the blankets.

By now it was late in the day, and it was decided that they would return to the lodge and wait for darkness before returning the bodies of the two men to the island.

Chapter 34

Breakfast was a peaceful affair that morning. Zachery and the Judge enjoyed a leisurely coffee and conversation. For once there was no intimidation or rude comments.

"Do you miss any of them?" asked Petrick.

"I must say, I don't know. In my own way, I'm as bad as they were! I guess I find that I come close to them in some respects."

"Do you think a person can change?" Petrick asked.

"*I think the difference between a rut and a grave, is depth.* I find being here has caused me to step back and take a long, hard look at myself. I don't like what I have done. I was becoming hard, cruel, uncaring and greedy: as these men have become, and that scares the shit out of me. And look at me! I more or less killed Chester, didn't I?"

"You *did* kill him, Zachery. There's no doubt there, but I think that if you hadn't done what you did, I strongly believe he would have done you worse!"

"You may be right, but still and all, don't you think that, eventually, we would have become one of them?" I think we're not the street fighters those men were. They came up the hard way, and we did not. We don't look over our shoulders like they do. I find their wariness and distrust quite fascinating. Did you notice that they seldom mention their past? It's like they constantly think they're being spied upon and afraid to reveal themselves. Of course, I'm afraid I was doing the same!"

"I agree with you there." Zachery was beginning to enjoy their honesty with one another. It was refreshing for some reason.

"I don't wish to pry, but what *exactly* would you do differently?" Asked the Judge.

"I suppose that, based on what we're talking about, I can hardly consider your question as prying. Let me tell you about my past. I own a pharmaceutical company, and I'm pretty good at it, but unfortunately I don't consider my end users enough. I'm into the trap of only making money. I've had people murdered, which is unforgivable. Also, I did some despicable things in order to pay off my gambling debts. I'm ashamed of my misdeeds and wish I could make amends. Looking back at my life, I'd make a lot of changes, if I had it to do all over again. Should I get the chance and if I ever get back home, I know I shall pay a dear price for my sins. I know now that I will never gamble again. I won't do a lot of things again!"

"What else would you do to make up for your sins, Zachery?"

Zachery thought about his answer long and hard before answering, and Petrick patiently waited for his reply. It took a few minutes for him to put together his answer.

"I would make a difference in my industry by only producing products that would benefit mankind, but at a more realistic cost, one that the average person could well afford. I'm sad to admit that price gouging is the norm in the pharmaceutical industry, and the product itself costs only pennies to produce. Our goal should be, to cure, not to addict and gouge. So many of us could live just as comfortably on millions rather than billions of dollars. I shall also continue to resist the greediness of the stock market. Our industry often uses the stock market to obtain venture capital, and we forget who we are working for: the public at large"

"Are you seriously telling me that you could pull all this off?"

"I could, and I would. I need both a cause and a cure for our industry."

Petrick smiled and nodded, lost in thought.

"What are you smiling at? You look like the cat that swallowed the canary."

"Since you've been so forthright with me, I'm going to share a few of my own plans I've been formulating. Up until the time of my captivity, I was a federally appointed judge, who forgot about justice and I turned bad. I took advantage of the system and I too descended into despicable practices. Let me explain. Our prison system is almost two hundred percent overpopulated. Our system of justice has gone sideways. Only the rich can afford the high caliber lawyer, whether crooked or honorable, to defend them and too many times, we use the faults of the system to get them off. And, in rare instances, when they are convicted, we are forced to give them a mere slap on the wrist.

The poor, who cannot afford proper legal council, are the people filling our prisons and who, more often receive the heavy sentencing. A lot of them are scapegoats of lazy and crooked law enforcement. They are the ones clogging our systems and costing society billions of dollars. Many of them are blacks and a lot of them falsely accused. Our justice system is pitifully clogged. We have failed our young people, who now think the whole justice system is a joke—and they're right. Our school system and parents deserve a failing grade for not getting our kids to follow and respect the law. Both parents are typically working full out, just to make ends meet and not spending nearly enough time with their kids."

"Anyway, I apologize for digressing. I allowed myself to become bored and bitter with the whole process, and drawn into the quagmire of justice instead of fighting the system and doing something about it. I took advantage of the system and started to accept bribes. After all, a lot of judges are doing it, so why shouldn't I? I've allowed my values to be flushed down the toilet. I even stooped to allow myself to get involved with child pornography, much of which was financed by the bribes I took. Whoever sent me here has done me a favor, in a lot of ways. Like you, I've stepped way back and took a long, hard look at myself. I don't want to wind up dead like the three buried on this island, without a chance to vindicate myself."

"That was quite a speech, your honor. But what do you think you can do about it?"

"I'll have no choice but to resign as a federal judge and I know I will have to face the wrath of the courts. I also know that in all probability, I will serve time in jail. If I can, I shall revert to being a simple lawyer once again. I'll donate my ill-gotten gains to help wrongly convicted people. I intend to do a lot of pro bono work too. I want to—*have* to—make the system stronger. I've badly neglected my wife, children and my parents and I'd like to do something about *that* too. I'm NOT a nice man!"

"What name do you go by?" asked Zachery. "Just between the two of us, of course."

"Why don't you call me by my first name. It's Allen, and I hope we can be friends. I don't have many of those! *My full name is Allen T Petrick*"

The two men shook on a newly found friendship. They both lacked friends, and this was another thing they both wanted to remedy, if and when they could reestablish themselves back into society. Zachery asked the Judge if he'd like to go for a walk on this beautiful clear day.

—

Matt, Charles and Jeff listened with great interest to the latest conversation in the island cabin. Matt was the first to break the silence.

"Since starting this crazy endeavor, I think I've changed my mind regarding the prison system in the US. I think handling prisoners is a very difficult challenge. We're just not equipped to handle prisoners of the caliber of these men. Five out of seven have died within a three week period and I am responsible, even though they brought it all on themselves. These types of characters need to be behind bars and guarded around the clock. This whole experiment has a bad effect on us all. I'd still like to hear your opinions or suggested options."

"I'd have to agree with you Matt," said Jeff. "I've felt absolutely powerless in preventing these deaths. I honestly never figured on the strength and determination that those dead guys possessed. The one that surprised me the most was Jazz escaping on that floating tree. That took a lot of guts and or, a bit of insanity thrown in!"

"Back in jolly old England," said Charles, "the justice system is no better. England is in the same straights, justice-wise, as in Canada and the US, and it's not about to change all that swiftly, if ever! I also agree that our system is absolutely clogged with the same stupid bureaucracy as it is here. Perhaps we should think a little more outside the box and somehow try and change the system without breaking the law and putting us all into this jeopardy. We may be able to influence some kind of change by using the satellite system we've devised. It's amazing what can be done if we put all our efforts into making a difference. Maybe by exposing more of the crookedness that is happening, just maybe, we might just make a *few* changes to the system. I feel, from now on, we should be more proactive in our approach."

"So Matt, what do we do with the two that are left?" asked Jeff.

"Believe me when I say, I've been considering that little dilemma, and I'm thinking that, based on the conversation we overheard just now, that it might be worthwhile to keep them here and let them serve out the full six months."

"I agree with you a hundred percent," said Jeff.

"I think we should close our operations here at the end of six months, do our dart trick with them and get back to our lives. I don't know about you two, but I'm bushed. This disaster has taken a lot out of us all."

—

Zachery and the judge soon discovered two inert figures under the blankets and knew what they would find. The presence of a shovel and another note, confirmed their suspicions. They read the note neatly tacked to the tree.

Hello again, assholes

Underneath the blankets you'll find the results of the two recent escapes. It won't be pretty, I can assure you. They didn't choose to listen to our warnings and succeeded in killing themselves. You two have two more burials to take care of. Your little island has quite the cemetery now. The dead out-number the living by more than three to one. Food for thought.

They walked over to the covered figures and drew back the blankets and were horrified at what had happened to the two men. Jack Mostar's throat had been torn open by what appeared to be some animal. He was cut, bruised and they could see that his arm was badly broken. He had come to a terrible end, and they wondered if they would *ever* discover what really happened to him.

Jazz had obviously drowned and probably been dragged underwater by the uprooted floating tree. Skin was missing from being dragged through the gravel river bottom. Abrasions and wounds covered his body. *Another horrible end!*

They decided to bury Jack Mostar and Jazz Hogue where they found them, as there wasn't room to bury them with the other three. They quickly set to work and were fortunate to dig into soft earth. They took turns digging, and it took three hours to complete the task before they could lower the two-blanketed figures into the cold ground. Another hour went by before they managed to shovel the dirt back into the graves. They neatly mounded the graves and both men sat down on boulders, to recover from their gruesome, arduous task.

Not a word was spoken the whole time. They slowly dragged themselves back to the cabin, listening to the relentless sound of the river as they walked.

Chapter 35

Six months had now passed. Winter had given way to spring. The two captives had remained undiscovered the entire time.

Another bright day greeted Zachery, as he emerged from the cabin to fetch water from the river. As he passed the cabin corner, he failed to notice the man who pointed a handgun at him. He felt the sting of a dart and fell soundlessly to the ground.

—

Matt rushed over to Zachery, dragged him behind the cabin and waited for Judge Petrick to emerge. Twenty minutes later, he did so, coming out to see what was taking his newfound friend so long. He was also darted and he too, fell unconscious. Jeff helped Matt carry the two men back to the boat.

Jeff had stayed behind the entire time at the hunting lodge and he was ready to return to civilization. Matt and the two pilots had landed the night before to fly everyone home, except the old caretaker, who continued to stay on.

They transported the two men to the hunting lodge and left Dan O'Malley to keep an eye on them. Matt, Jeff, and Bob Cummings returned to the island and spent the rest of the day removing all evidence of what had taken place. Leftover food supplies, bedding, clothing and all eavesdropping equipment was dismantled and carried back to the boat. They walked to the first gravesite with shovels and quickly dug two new graves. They removed the rocks covering Harry Blankford (Bear), Chester Bennett and gently lowered their remains into the freshly dug holes. They refilled the graves and tamped down the soil, erasing all evidence of what had taken place. Rocks were strewn over the three graves. Anyone visiting the island would find only an empty cabin.

By the time they drove the boat back to the hunting lodge, it was getting dark.

The two unconscious men were carried to the secret compartment of the Learjet. The lodge was put into proper order and the computers were taken to the Learjet. They decided to fly directly to New York and return the Judge to his home. They would then fly to Dallas and return Zachery to his office. A long flight awaited them. They strapped themselves in as preparations were made for takeoff and as the plane lifted off, they looked down at the tiny island. The full moon illuminated the now deserted island. So much had happened there during the six months. *It felt like a lifetime.*

Matt sat back in his seat. "I don't know about you Jeff, but this has been quite an experience, but it will never be repeated, nor will I ever forget the island experiment. What about you?"

"I think I'm ready to rejoin society now," said Jeff. "Strangely, I feel a form of justice has taken place here. It will be interesting to see how the remaining two will make out when they wake up back on their home turf tomorrow. Do you think that you'll ever do anything similar to this again?"

Matt shook his head. "I don't think so. I think that from now on, I'll take a different approach. I'm disappointed in myself for not anticipating what has happened. The whole thing has been a fiasco! I thought I could have made more of a difference. I do, however, think that Judge Petrick and Zachery have learned something valuable here and will remember it for the rest of their lives. The two have certainly became good friends. The two men sat back, relieved to be heading back to normal living once again.

Matt was restless and found himself reassessing how he would continue to help rid the scum of society. Next time, he would operate within the perimeters of the law while doing so. *Well, almost!!*

He also found himself thinking how profoundly he was missing his family and retreated to a seat in the back of the plane and called home.

To his delight, Sam answered the phone and sounded much better and seemed to be rebounding well, after what had happened to him, more than half a year ago. Father and son talked for fifteen minutes about things inconsequential. Sam also talked of his dead friend and what he had learned from that devastating drug experience. He mentioned that his school was now pretty much drug free and how some of the parents and some ex-army volunteers were working together to keep it from reoccurring.

Matt's spirits were lifted by Sam's enthusiasm. Mia was next to speak and was telling him about how she was helping her mother at the marina. One of the dolphins had given her a kiss the day before. She couldn't wait to go to get through school and be a marine biologist just like Mom. Matt couldn't wait to see his children again.

Matt asked Mia to put her mom on the line. He could feel the relief in her voice as soon as she picked up the phone.

"Matt, are you alright? I haven't heard from you in days," said Kirsten, "that is so unlike you."

"I've been cleaning up a few things on the island and to say the least, I'm relieved to say that I'm pulling the plug on the island thing. It was an awful experience. I still want to make a difference though, because of all the corruption in our world. I'll just have to find a different avenue from now on."

"Do you know when you'll be home again, Matt? We all miss you terribly."

"I'll be home in a few days. There are a few things I have to finish. I love you Kirsten and I miss you all. See you soon."

He had two more calls to make. Then had a couple of letters to write.

Chapter 36

Judge Allen T. Petrick was slow to awaken. He found himself groggy and very hungry. Everything was somehow different: brighter and it smelt a whole lot better. Then he realized with a start that he was in his own bed. He was home! His first thought was the sheer pleasure of freedom, and then, strangely, a foreboding and a sense of loneliness starting to set in. Surely he didn't miss the island! *Did he?* Or did he miss the company of Zachery, his newfound friend?

The judge slowly sat up on the edge of the bed. The sun was just starting rise. An envelope was on his nightstand and neatly printed was the now familiar heading.

> Hello for the final time Asshole! At least I hope this will be the final time!
>
> As you can plainly see, you're off the island and home in your own bed. I firmly believe that your life will eventually get better. I may be wrong, and if I am, you'll be a permanent residence of the island, but this time with absolutely no reprieve. I'm sure the police and the law system will soon deal with you further and you sorely deserve it.
>
> I'd strongly advise you to step away from the awful exploitation of children with regard to pornography and get yourself some form of counseling. I'd also suggest that you

seriously take steps toward doing some good in our society, after you've been suitably punished. Ask yourself the question; do I really like the position of being a judge? There's a hell of a lot better ways for you to effect some positive change in our society! Please think seriously about this. In the interim, why don't you make peace with your parents and give some recognition to your wife. I've found out she's a special woman. She must be, to put up with an asshole like you! I wonder how she reacted when she found out about your pornography habits? Hug your kids, and tell them you love them for Christ sake!

I've taken the liberty of enclosing the address and phone number of Zachery Melcan.

He slowly reread the letter a second time. He considered waking his wife in her room—at least he hoped she was still there. He had lots to think about and some serious changes to make in his life. With grim determination, he picked up the phone and called a lawyer.

—

Fifteen hundred and sixty miles away, Zachery Melcan woke up on his office couch. It took him a few minutes to realize where he was. He was back and a bit confused. He didn't know what to do. His mind flashed back to the island and all that had taken place there. It felt like a lifetime had passed, but it had lasted only six months. ONLY! He knew he would never again be the same. He sat up and glanced around his neat office. It was dark. A lamp had been turned on in one corner and an envelope was leaning up against it. His full name was written in large black letters. He smiled at the familiar neat lettering written on it.

Hello for the final time asshole! At least I hope this will be the last time!

What are you going to do now? You've certainly fucked things up in your life, but you made your own choices. Fuck up again and you'll wind up back on the island for good!

You and I both know that you're going to be severally punished for what you've done and you deserve it! I urge you to call the police and come clean. Be honest for once, asshole! If and when you're suitably punished, why not do some good for a change?

Why not help people, rather profit from their health miseries. I urge you to eventually start creating products that will genuinely help improve the quality of life for people in ill health. For once in your miserable existence, why don't you consider taking some leadership in your industry and lead by example? I can assure you, in the long run, you'll be more successful and respected than you've ever dreamed possible.

I've pulled a few strings to help you get back on the straight and narrow, but I'm sure you still won't be in the clear. YES, I'm sure you'll still be punished; however, as far as I'm concerned, you've recently learned some valuable lessons about the consequences of wrongdoing. I've paid off your gambling debts and I suggest you forget about ever trying the gambling route again. Get some counseling if you have to!

Get yourself a good woman and make amends to the people who have helped you in your life. Time to start living the good life. I'll help when I can, from time to time, but you and I will never meet! I've taken the liberty to include the address of your newfound friend. His full name is Judge Allen T. Petrick, and he lives in New York. You two are in a great position to help each other, believe me.

Zachery was struck hard after reading the letter, and was sorry he would never meet the man who had taught him so much in so short a time. It was now time to pay the piper and to make changes in his life. First, a phone call phone to the police and make a full confession. Time to pay the piper! He had the sudden urge to call Evelyn Twain. *He was alive!*

Epilogue

Matt chambers soon learned that he had accomplished more than he expected. Drug use in the schools in Seattle continued to decline. The school volunteers were indeed making a difference and had managed to put the run on drug pushers in a few schools. *It was a start!* Even the kids were cooperating by networking with the authorities, and because of this, arrests were being made.

The court system in Washington State was finally starting to flex its muscles in regards to drug dealing. Charges were being strongly enforced, and stiff sentences were quickly carried out. The penalties were stiffening. A work camp for accused drug dealers was being built in an inaccessible mountainous area in the Washington wilderness. The work camp would be void of any frills, which would mean less expense on taxpayers. The message would soon go out. TRAFFIC DRUGS AND YOU"LL PAY THE PRICE!

It was also being considered that ex army veterans would be hired to police it. Prisoners would work during the week and all had to participate in a school program during the weekend. Visitation by outsiders was off limits. Word would soon get out and drug pushers would become harder to find. Drug cartels were being shaken up and were beginning to look over their shoulders.

Seattle was setting the example for the world, and the world would soon start to pay attention. There was even rumors that gun control was coming to Washington State. Gun lobbyists were becoming alarmed by this and were making outrageous demands on crooked government officials. Certain politicians were beginning to get nervous. The public was starting to speak, and Congress was starting to listen. Matt's spark had started a small fire, and he would continue to add fuel to that fire.

Charles Freemont continued his work in New York with Secure Satellite Security. He was going to light a few fires too.

Jeff Harrigan was sent to Dallas to open a new Southern branch of Secure Satellite Security. In time, he too would become instrumental in making some powerful changes and would soon be making a few changes to his own life.

As for Judge Allen T. Petrick, he resigned his judgeship and was sentenced to three year in jail and was kicked out of the legal profession. After serving half of this sentence, he was released on good behavior. While incarcerated, he had helped some of the prisoners, who had been wrongly accused and managed to get two of them released.. His wife left him, but his children forgave him, after he had served his time in jail. His parents came back into his life and together they would help him re enter society once again. Ex judge Petrick vowed that he would somehow rectify his wrongs and do some good in his small world. When released from prison, one of the first things he did, was to get himself some professional counseling

Zachery Melcan was given a life sentence for the murders of the two researchers. He signed over what was left of his company to Evelyn Twain. An anonymous contribution enabled her to achieve her goals. She would go on to become a leader in the pharmaceutical world. Evelyn decided that only safe drugs would be manufactured at reduced costs to the public. This was producing a lot of static in the pharmaceutical world, but she would weather the storm and was making some much-needed changes to the industry. She was able to convince Jessica Rawlins to head the research department once again. This was a move that Zachery was happy to endorse.

Zachery had two regular visitors while he served his sentence. *Evelyn Twain and his friend, Allen T. Petrick.*

Barney and Nina were married and would soon give birth to a son. Matt had some interesting proposals for the both of them in the near future. Barney's sister, Sara Bennett and her son Jeremy were advised of her husband's death (Chester Bennett), and were greatly relieved. But they both decided to retain their new identities.

Wes Harrison managed to convict mob chief Gino Danelli and his gang, and they would be out of circulation for a long time. Wes never made the connection as to who was instrumental in getting the gang arrested.

Sean Mallory was killed in prison by one of Gino Danelli's gang -members.

CPSIA information can be obtained at www.ICGtesting.com
Printed in the USA
LVOW13*0715200314

378118LV00001B/1/P